Short Cat Tales

AMY KRISTOFF

Deer Run Press
Cushing, Maine

Copyright © 2023 Amy Kristoff.

All rights reserved. No part this book may be reproduced or transmitted in any form or by any means, electronic or mechanical, including photocopying, recording, or by any information storage and retrieval system, without written permission from the copyright owner.

This is a work of fiction. Names, characters, places and incidents either are the product of the author's imagination or are used fictitiously, and any resemblance to any actual persons (living or dead), events, or locales is entirely coincidental.

Library of Congress Card Number: 2023947525

ISBN: 978-1-937869-21-2

First Printing, 2023

Published by
Deer Run Press
8 Cushing Road
Cushing, ME 04563

Contents

Sunny//1
The Cat Lady//12
Disinherited Son//19
The Cat Tale Pond//27
Trinket//39
Don't Let the Cat Out!//45
One Crazy Former Cat Owner//52
One Lying Cat Owner//60
Here, Kitty, Kitty//64
Tammy the Social Scaredy-Cat//68
The Cat Becomes Family//73
The Cat Writer//82

Sunny

Downtown Sand Springs, Florida, was the site of a weekly "open market" on Saturday mornings, rain or shine. A portion of Main Street was in fact closed to traffic for part of the day. Occasionally it was raining, but all the vendors erected their displays beneath an awning of some sort if not an actual tent, so there was always a sizable turnout. Knowing as much was what compelled Madge Gallen, the director of Charlotte County Animal Shelter, to initiate organizing an adoption event one Saturday in early March, specifically for the "older set" of cats and dogs at the shelter. If attendees of the weekly flea market-type event were in the mood to buy, maybe they would also be in the mood to adopt an older, hard to place pet.

Julia Hart wouldn't be exaggerating if she admitted to practically living for her foray amongst the offerings at Sand Springs' weekly en plein air market, as there was an ever-changing list of vendors. On the morning in question, it looked like rain when she left the house but didn't bother to even throw a windbreaker in her purse, "in case." Nothing peeved her like rain pelting her back, especially if all she had on was a T-shirt, as she did on this particular day, with the temperature about 75 degrees. Julia lived in "The Sunshine State"(?) because her beloved husband, Steven, always wanted to move here after retiring as an optometrist. Barely four years after the move, he died in his sleep. Again and again she was told by family, friends and acquaintances, "At least he didn't suffer!" and every time she wanted to reply, "What about me?" It never occurred to Julia to return to Ohio, where they had owned a beautiful house on two acres in Sharon Center. It was as if she was determined to fulfill a wish of Steven's to live in Florida "until the end," never mind the fact she missed the four distinct seasons and wasn't a fan of year-round humidity.

It had already been almost two years since he passed, and in the meantime, Julia's (and Steven's) twelve-year-old Pembroke Welsh Corgi, Lottie, passed away too. Devastated wasn't a strong enough word to describe how Julia felt after that second low blow. Lottie had previously been diagnosed with an inoperable tumor, and the veterinarian had indicated she "might go anytime," but it was still a shock to have her collapse after eating lunch one day. Julia was still numb after losing Steven unexpectedly, a man who neither smoked nor drank and whose worst habit was playing golf every day on the course their house overlooked, specifically the 13th tee of "Coral Reef," part of "Coral Reef Country Club and Villas" (two-story townhouses were also added in the last half dozen years, making use of land that might have otherwise accommodated another course, albeit one that was only nine holes).

Arriving at downtown Sand Springs after a ten-minute drive, Julia parked at the far north end of Main Street, in a large public parking lot. It was still early enough in the morning, there were metered spaces available that were closer, but she was here to browse and bargain-hunt, so how could she justify feeding a meter to park for an hour or two? Besides, she happened to like walking, which made it easier to stay in shape. Since Lottie was no longer Julia's walking companion, she became resigned to living alone and doing all her daily activities by herself.

The sky finally darkened to the point rain was inevitable, and Julia had just reached the start of where the vendor tents and awnings were set up, both on the sidewalk and in

Short Cat Tales

the street, leaving a passageway down the middle of Main. A few errant raindrops landed on her before she ducked under a large white tent on her left, having no idea what was displayed underneath it. Then she saw a light blue plastic banner hung from one side of a long folding table to the other, with the following in bold black letters across the front, variously-colored cat and dog silhouettes around it: "Charlotte County Animal Shelter Emergency Adoption Event!" Seated at the table was a woman busily typing on a laptop, wearing a green, button-down, short-sleeved shirt with the name of the shelter inscribed on the left pocket. She looked up to greet Julia, who nodded and said hello. Julia just wanted to stay out of the rain, which would probably be stopping in a few minutes. In the meantime, the spacious tent was very accommodating, and while looking around, she realized there were several sets of eyes of both cats and dogs watching her, the cages for the latter to her right, stacked three-high and four across, the cages for the former in front of her, stacked three-high and five across. A quick glance at the dogs appeared to reveal there was nothing but medium to large-sized dogs. Stubby-legged Lottie had spoiled Julia with her proportions, as she was medium-sized but short in stature, perfect for any living situation.

Julia looked in the direction of the cat cages, and her blue eyes met the green ones of a cute, delicate-looking black cat, on the top level. Julia went up to the cage and peered inside, and the cat meowed. The laminated card on the front of the cage indicated her name was "Sunny," a spayed shorthair who was twelve. No wonder it was an emergency pet adoption event. These poor animals didn't have much time, no matter what!

It seemed only fair (to the animal shelter and the animals themselves) to give all the cats and dogs a once-over, so Julia did, starting with the latter. One of the dogs, "Buddy," a neutered terrier mix, vaguely resembled a Pembroke Welsh Corgi, with a fox-like face and oversized ears, as well as a tan and white coat. The similarities ended there, given his long legs and tail as well as very short, wiry-looking fur. Julia would have considered giving him a chance, except he was fourteen! She vowed then and there if she adopted an elderly dog or cat, she (or he) couldn't be older than twelve.

Julia returned to looking at the cats, and it was difficult to focus on any cat but Sunny. She meowed at Julia a couple more times, apparently determined to get her attention. A cat! Julia would have found that inclination much more likely from a dog, yet Sunny and she had some sort of connection, there was no denying it.

Julia turned around to ask the lady at the table, on the computer, about Sunny, but she had already gotten up, evidently having witnessed the mutual interest between Sunny and Julia.

"She's a real sweetheart," the woman remarked. "I'm Sue, by the way."

"I'm Julia," she said. "I've been a dog owner for years, and I haven't lived with a cat since we took care of my grandmother Terrell's cat, Precious, when I was young. She was my mom's mom, who'd died alone in her house, sitting in her favorite chair, and the cat was found in her lap. I get a chill every time I tell anyone that. I guess because it's touching yet heartbreaking."

"It certainly is. Thank you for sharing. Would you happen to currently have any pets at home?"

"No, and I live alone," Julia replied. Then she briefly explained "the why" behind as much, and Sue appeared ready to sob. Julia definitely had tears in her eyes, herself!

Sue proceeded to explain how bossy Sunny was toward other cats, and she had in fact recently been adopted into a household with two cats and a dog, the cats being the ones who prompted her return, thanks to how intimidating she was! Julia thought that was funny, considering Sunny couldn't have weighed more than three or four pounds and had an adorable, kittenish face.

Short Cat Tales

Sue added, "I don't know Sunny's whole story prior to when she was originally brought to the shelter, but I believe she was the only pet in the house of an elderly widow."

"My daughter will think I've lost it if I adopt a cat because I don't like when they jump on counters and other places. I see that at someone's house and think, 'Not for me!'"

"I was going to ask if your daughter lived with you, but you told me you live alone."

"She lives in Ohio, where we're from, but she visits me once or twice a year and will be doing so, soon. She absolutely despises cats and is a neat-freak, so she may end up staying in a hotel if I have cat-company. It wouldn't be the worst thing because she complains I don't keep the house clean enough. I happen to prefer the lived-in look."

"Pet owners have to be realistic," Sue said, "and pet owners' loved ones have to be understanding."

Julia was ready to take Sunny home, but Sue said it was "the shelter's policy" the two get to know one another a little bit, first. She also explained there was a small enclosure with "tall, unclimbable sides" for doing just that, on the other side of the cat cages. Julia hadn't seen it and had expected Sue to throw Sunny in a cardboard box with air holes and call it a day. Once Julia got Sunny settled at the house, she intended to go back out and purchase some cat-related items. It was exciting to have a new companion to get to know, and Sunny had already made Julia realize loneliness had pervaded her life more than she'd been aware.

There was genuine concern about Julia's daughter Nicole's reaction to Sunny, however. Not only did Nicole detest cats, there was a determination in her to never be happy for her mom or just be happy in general. She didn't inherit that attitude from Julia, but she might have gotten it from Steven's mother, Alana. Julia had chalked up Alana's behavior to the fact she had numerous health issues, was on several medications, and above all enjoyed being mean to a daughter-in-law she didn't like, namely Julia. After Alana's passing, Julia came to the conclusion the woman was probably never happy and didn't want anyone else to be, either.

After the adoption paperwork was completed, Julia carried Sunny back to her car in a cardboard box with airholes, just like she'd imagined. She was also given a sample package of dry cat food. Under the circumstances, it was helpful Sunny didn't weigh much. Since it had stopped raining, at least there was no chance of the cardboard getting soggy.

Julia was so excited to be taking her newly-adopted cat home, she couldn't help talking to her as they walked, not caring who heard: "See Sunny, it stopped raining! That's all thanks to you and that name of yours!" Meanwhile, Sunny was completely silent for a change, which Julia guessed was better than if she was making some of the hideous sounds cats were capable of.

***

"You what?" Nicole exclaimed into the phone that evening, talking to her mother, who called to tell Nicole what she did that day. Nicole initially wanted to blame her mother's latest action on senility, but she was most likely simply lonely. Her mother had more friends back here in Ohio than she did in her adopted state of Florida, but she refused to return. Speaking of adopting, that was exactly what her mother did, in regard to a runty, old black cat, a picture of which was texted to Nicole immediately after they spoke. Receiving that photo was amazing onto itself because her mother hated technology, even something as simple as texting. Maybe her mother really was losing it. Nicole was ready to lose it because she wanted to visit her next month, but she'd already decided the cat was too grubby-looking to be under the same roof as herself. She might have to cut her stay by a day or two and make a reservation at a hotel, which would have to be five-star because anything cheap always seemed less clean, although there was probably little difference between any hotel room deemed "clean," no matter what the rate was.

The worst part of the whole scenario was her mother sounded happier than she'd been in years. It was understandable she was depressed following the sudden death of her husband, Nicole's dad, so she wasn't exactly fun to be around. Still, did she have to spring out of nowhere and be this happy? It was going to be harder to endure her than when she was in the doldrums. At least Nicole could kind of relate, insofar as why her mother had been depressed. Nicole always got along with her dad and still couldn't quite believe he died "just like that." It wasn't fair she didn't at least get to say good-bye.

Whenever Nicole visited her mother, she typically took a rideshare from the airport and then went places with her mother in her car or else borrowed her car to go somewhere alone. If "forced" to stay at a hotel, Nicole would have to take a rideshare to her mother's in order to borrow her car! It was all a stupid cat's fault, any of this even had to be considered!

Nicole didn't take as much time off from her job as an optometrist as she was allowed. Visiting her mother was an excuse to get away, and it was relatively inexpensive. Again, all that was potentially about to change, thanks to a dirty old cat. Nicole wanted to save her money so she could eventually open her own optometry office, versus remain where she was, working at a facility with several optometrists. It was a pleasant environment but had become too impersonal for both the employees and the patients, thanks to the large volume of appointments. It was a shame she hadn't decided to be an optometrist before her father sold his business and retired, but she had a stint as an interior decorator, first. At the time, she was engaged to a home builder in the Cincinnati area, and she did all the decorating and staging of the model homes in his developments, in addition to doing freelance work. The end of her interior decorator career coincided with the end of her engagement, which became inevitable. She'd needed a fresh start, so she went back to school.

Nicole decided to check online for hotel room availability, not concern herself with the rates for the time being. She might be forced to rely on someone canceling a reservation, given how comparatively last-minute her plans were. The worst case scenario was she had to stay at her mother's after all and tolerate a disgusting old cat.

***

It seemed to take Sunny no time at all to make herself at home, although she had already been with Julia for three weeks. Julia was having a harder time living with a cat than she expected, meaning she would be doing a task of some sort and happen to look up and see Sunny as if for the first time! Julia would ask her how she was doing, and Sunny would meow in response. In that moment, Julia would be so grateful for the company (despite the initial surprise), she'd sometimes weep! Even though she no longer had a walking companion, Julia appreciated the kind of friendship Sunny provided. She was indeed a special cat, and Julia credited Sunny's former owner(s) for some of that.

Monday afternoon of next week (it was Tuesday) Nicole was coming to visit. She'd tried to make a hotel reservation but couldn't seem to find a room for her four-day stay. Julia was worried Nicole was going to ruin everything because of resenting Sunny. It seemed ridiculous to think like that, but Nicole could be ridiculous! At thirty-five, she had an excellent salary as an optometrist and basically "had it made." Nevertheless, she could be so selfish, critical, and ungrateful. It was terrible for "Nicole's mother" to declare as much, but at least it helped explain why Nicole had yet to marry!

Julia had taken to walking on the cart paths for the back nine at Coral Reef, versus walking around the neighborhood, as she did previously, whether alone or with Lottie. She made

Short Cat Tales

a point of getting up early to do so, before the golfers started playing, even though none started on the back nine first, at least not when she'd been out there. She'd begun this "ritual" after bringing Sunny home because the cat had immediately taken to sitting on the cushioned bench in the sun room's bay window, which overlooked the small in-ground pool in the back yard and the golf course, beyond. If Nicole "found out" Julia took a walk as early as she did (and the reason behind it, that Sunny was [possibly] watching her), she'd think her mother was crazy. Julia wasn't bothered by that, but what did bother her was the fact Nicole would in turn take the liberty of cruelly deriding her. Naturally, if Nicole was called out on her behavior, she would claim to be "kidding," nothing more. It was up to Nicole if her four-day stay seemed like four weeks, for everyone. Julia would have to tell her to plan on staying at a hotel next time.

It never occurred to Julia to sell the house and find a place that wasn't on a golf course, since she didn't golf, never had. The membership dues at Coral Reef Country Club allowed access to not only the course but two restaurants and a spa, so it wasn't as if Julia didn't make some use of the amenities. Ever since Steven passed, it was hard to get excited about cooking just for herself, so at least once a week she went to dinner at the clubhouse, sometimes dressing up to dine at the fancier of the two restaurants, "Mais Oui." She liked the area where she lived and wasn't interested in starting over someplace else. Even though she didn't have any neighbors who were also close friends, the residents always waved and/or said hello to one another and so did she.

Julia did have one neighbor a few houses down, Patty Silver, who was a "good acquaintance." She too was a widow and owned a female Sheltie named "Lady." Shortly before Julia and Steven moved into their house, Patty lost another Sheltie, "Dino," to an alligator, who was in the pond just to the right of the thirteenth green (where there should have been a sand trap, Steven often complained). Anyway, Dino had somehow gotten out of the wrought-iron fenced back yard (all the yards that were adjacent to the course were fenced) and was swallowed by the alligator, who sprang out of the pond, as witnessed by a foursome of men, one Sunday morning. If that had happened to Lottie, Julia would have moved. Patty was evidently more resilient than Julia and got another dog, instead. Not to be flippant, but Patty was an avid golfer, so maybe she was better-equipped to keep the calamity in perspective.

Patty had invited Julia over for coffee on a couple of occasions, and Julia had reciprocated the gesture. Patty lost her husband, Tom, several years ago after a long battle with cancer. Their two adult sons still lived in the area and had yet to marry, nor did they have any kids. That sounded so bleak until Julia realized her own, personal plight wasn't any better! Nicole had (proudly) made it clear a number of times she had no interest in being a mother, although she didn't rule out becoming a stepmother if she married a guy who was completely obsessed with her. That was the only way she'd tolerate dealing with his ex-wife and living with their rug rats. Julia used to become distraught, listening to Nicole talk like that, but she had learned to not only accept this attitude of her daughter's but to embrace it. At least she was being honest.

Just as Julia was about to get some housework out of the way, her phone rang. Any excuse would do, to avoid vacuuming. Fortunately, Sunny was very accepting of the sound of it, and if she was taking a nap in the sun room when Julia turned it on, she'd sleep right through the whole thing. Granted, Julia skipped vacuuming in that room if Sunny was already in there, but it had a wide entryway with no door, so the vacuum could easily be heard in there, no matter what room Julia was vacuuming in. (The white stucco, ranch-style house was "only" about 1700 square feet.)

None other than Patty called, inviting Julia over for coffee. Saying yes meant more procrastination of housework,

Short Cat Tales

but it was probably better to put if off until the day of Nicole's arrival. Otherwise everything would have to be done over again, thanks to overly-meticulous Nicole. Julia couldn't figure out who in the family shared her daughter's fanaticism about neatness. Anyway, Julia told Patty about Sunny and asked if she wanted to come over and have coffee at her place instead and see Sunny.

"Oh, that's all right," Patty said. "I'm not much for cats."

Julia took that to mean no, she wasn't interested in seeing Sunny. Julia felt foolish for assuming Patty liked cats because she had a dog. Now Julia was in a quandary because she was disgusted and didn't want to see Patty at all —ever again! There went Julia's relationship with one "good acquaintance," who was anti-cat or might as well have been.

Simply put, Sunny was a special cat who had saved Julia from her debilitating loneliness. The bond they shared was the only thing that mattered.

The Cat Lady

I never thought I'd return home to Clarmore, Indiana to attend the funeral for my best friend in junior and senior high school, Janelle Holmby, when she was "only" 55. It wasn't young, but her death was nonetheless jarring. Although we were no longer close, that was first and foremost because she remained in the area where we grew up, while I attended college in the desert Southwest and moved there. We talked on the phone occasionally and exchanged birthday as well as Christmas cards. As a registered nurse at Indianapolis General Hospital, she met a lot of people, but she never found someone to marry, what she always wanted. She succumbed to an aggressive illness that was discovered when she went to a routine dentist's appointment. Her mother, Beth, was noticeably distraught when disclosing the news over the phone, but I made her feel slightly better when I volunteered to pay my respects in person. Meanwhile, my personal life was a shambles after recently ending an unhappy, eight-year marriage. So much for waiting until later in life to marry Mr. Right. I gave up on relationships and vowed to stay focused on my work at a Scottsdale, Arizona art and antiquities auction house.

Flying from Phoenix Sky Harbor Airport to Indianapolis International in mid-July, I traveled from dry heat to humidity. I rented a car for the twenty-five minute drive south of Indianapolis to Clarmore and was amazed at how much the area had grown in the past thirty-seven years, although that was quite a lot of time. It only seemed like it hadn't been that

Short Cat Tales

long. Still, I thought everyone wanted to get away from the Midwest. My parents, Duane and Shirley, ended up following me to the Phoenix area a few years ago, eliminating any reason to return home. Mom in particular was glad to have finally left. There was a side of me that was looking forward to visiting the place where I grew up, "one last time." I would be attending the wake that evening and the funeral in the morning, before flying back to Phoenix. It was early afternoon, and I intended to spend some time driving around, passing my former home and haunts, the latter of which included "The House on Bunker Hill," although it was no more, having recently burned to the ground. At the time, it was commonly called "The Cat Lady's House," although it was hardly fair to accuse the resident, Marie Harem, of hoarding cats. All she really did was humanely take in every unwanted cat that was callously dumped at the end of desolate Bunker Hill Road. Meanwhile, my mother knew Marie and her father, Vance, the latter of whom formerly used the building for a private girls' reform school. It became so popular there was a waiting list. Parents must have signed up their daughters before they got into trouble, planning on the worst. After all, the attendees weren't "of age" indefinitely. My mother never explained how she knew Vance Morgan and his daughter. Marie was widowed at 30, due to an unfortunate accident her husband, Harold, had. He left his wife taken care of financially, and since Marie's father had paid off the mortgage on the five-acre property before retiring, Marie was free to become an eccentric, reclusive caretaker of both the place where she lived and all its feline inhabitants. Never ambitious but at least vibrant, Marie became a shell of herself once her husband unexpectedly died. It happened one winter day as he attempted to clean some snow off the roof where it had drifted over a section of gutter. He carelessly tried to access the drift via the second-story porch, using the wide wooden railing to stand on while holding a snow shovel. Almost immediately he lost his balance and fell on the con-

Amy Kristoff

crete walkway below, where there was no cushion of snow because he had just shoveled it.

Supposedly as many as a hundred cats lived with Marie by the time I dropped off "the last meal" to her and later that week, left to start college in Arizona. Having so many cats couldn't have solved her loneliness dilemma because she always had a haunted look in her eyes, not that I saw her every time I delivered food, which I did about three times a month. My mother would call to let her know when I was coming (with Janelle), and I would knock on the front door upon my arrival if she didn't open the door once I reached the sagging wooden stoop. Inevitably a couple cats would make a run for it, but she didn't seem to notice or care. None ever appeared to be starving, but neither did any of them look robust and healthy. Other times I would have to knock, and from within she would say, "Please leave it by the door. Thank you." I would do as I was told and respond, "You're welcome," but it seemed insensitive to simply depart on my final day, so I lingered for a few seconds. Janelle asked me what was wrong once I got back in my mom's car, having evidently witnessed me hesitating. I told her I felt badly, leaving Marie alone in that big building with no one to keep her company but a bunch of abandoned cats. I'd previously referred to the former school as "The House on Bunker Hill," but its actual name was "Clarmore Girls' Academy," which sounded like a depressing place to be holed up in, alone. Although I didn't tell Janelle this, I wished I'd said good-bye to Marie. Janelle had little sympathy for Marie and was convinced Marie could leave the premises for good when she'd had enough, letting the cats fend for themselves, especially since most of them had been "given to her." Janelle might have been sick of riding along with me on these jaunts, but she never told me she had something better to do. I was an obedient daughter, but the truth of the matter was the second I had my driver's license, I was always looking for an excuse to go somewhere in my mom's car. (The meal delivery was taken

Short Cat Tales

over by my mom until she moved to Arizona.) I never asked her why she always had me take care of delivering what she cooked. Wouldn't she want to do so, herself? Neither did I ask, "Why Marie as the recipient?" because I assumed my mom felt sorry for her, as did everyone in Clarmore, except Janelle and anyone who had burdened her with an unwanted cat. If I had "done the math" regarding Marie's age versus my mom's, I could have considered the possibility they were related, as in Marie was my half-sister. I wouldn't have been able to handle it back then.

It was tempting to describe Marie as a rich eccentric, but when she had been deeded the former school to live in, there was an understanding from her father, she too would do something with the property, whose square footage was never confirmed. I heard it was as "little" as seven-thousand square feet and as much as fifteen. It was probably closer to the former size. Thanks to her husband, there were plans to turn the building into a writer's and artist's retreat as well as an art gallery, given the many large, light-filled rooms, the commanding views inside and out, and its central location in regard to the rest of the country. Since there were steep drop-offs on three sides of the five-acre property, no land development would ever ruin the benefit of living at the end of Bunker Hill Road. Harold grew up in New York City, and both of his parents were playwrights, well-known in East Coast theater circles. Harold had a couple well-received suspense novels published by a major publishing house, but he felt like name recognition was the only thing that got him the book contracts, not his talent. He wanted to do something on his own and make his parents as well as his father-in-law proud, but it wasn't meant to be. Marie's father passed away when she was 35, and she was still deeply grieving the death of her husband. She'd lost her mother, Katherine, to cancer when she, Marie, was in elementary school. Her aunt Edna, her father's sister, helped raise her, but doing so wasn't her aunt's idea of personal fulfillment, having never married nor

Amy Kristoff

had kids of her own, "by choice." That was Aunt Edna's supposed reason for being so aloof toward Marie. Nevertheless, Aunt Edna was willing to do her older brother a favor since he was busy running the school and didn't have much time for his daughter. Or that was his excuse.

To reach my destination I had to pass through meager downtown Clarmore, which had gotten even "smaller" with age, and continue south on Route 47, which didn't pass any more rural areas until about a mile before reaching Bunker Hill Road. In the meantime there were a number of new subdivisions, the residents forced to drive north through Clarmore and continue toward Indianapolis to do most of their shopping. Once I turned east on Bunker Hill Road, it was like I had stepped back in time to when I drove my mom's Oldsmobile Ciera to deliver her home-cooked meals to Marie Harem.

Bunker Hill Road was paved and flat for about a third of a mile, with soybean fields on either side. Then it abruptly ascended and shortly thereafter, the pavement became very rutty, as if the job of finishing smoothing the blacktop had been permanently put on hold. There were more open fields, but after a couple hundred yards, towering oak trees appeared on either side, broken up by a winding gravel driveway on the left and on the right, with big, worn-looking, metal mailboxes in front of each. I wondered if the same people and/or families lived at the residences as when I used to drive past?

More ascending lay ahead, and Bunker Hill Road became ruttier still. Then it curved slightly south and leveled off, the same point at which the pavement ended and was replaced by packed gravel that was like concrete. Finally there was a large clearing, and the site of what was once "The House on Bunker Hill" came into view. Fifty more feet and I drove into what was formerly the circular gravel driveway in front of the building, which still had some gravel mostly hidden by dirt. There was a flag pole in the middle, surrounded by stacked cement blocks, which evidently survived not only the fire but the bulldozer that leveled the ground afterward. I didn't see any harm in getting out for a couple minutes (despite being a trespasser), so I did, drawn by the eeriness and compelled to sit down on the cement blocks. My mom kept in touch with some friends that still lived in Clarmore, so she was always up to date on all the current events. Although arson wasn't the suspected cause of the fire, there was an ongoing investigation of some sort. Since Marie had passed away before it happened, she was free of any blame.

Looking at the sky, it was starting to become cloudy, and there was a good chance of rain by evening. Humid though it was, a cool breeze "up here," made it more comfortable. It really did feel like the top of the world, and I completely understood why Marie Harem remained here, despite her husband's unfortunate demise.

Marie spent a few months in an assisted living facility before her death, as her health only declined more rapidly once she was removed from familiar surroundings. I had to wonder who "rescued" her? Perhaps she summoned help because she could no longer take care of herself. Anyway, she was told the cats would be taken to various animal shelters in the area, and she needn't worry about them. It was a good thing she probably didn't because many of the cats were difficult to locate, once several animal rescue teams were allowed to access the building. They got a grand total of about 25 cats. That was still a decent number, but it was nowhere near the hundred-plus mark, what had been anticipated. There were probably more volunteers than cats, as it turned out.

The wind started to increase, and I looked upward at the sky again, thinking maybe there was a black cloud overhead, and it was about to pour down rain, one of those sudden, drenching bursts, but no. If anything, the sun was trying to shine through the clouds. I continued to sit there, thinking about everything, and it remained entirely possible Marie

Amy Kristoff

Harem was my half-sister. If that was too much to handle all those years ago, it was actually even harder at this point in time. Given both my parents' fragile health, particularly my mom's, it was impossible to ask her if I was right to suspect what I did. She would most likely deny it, even if it was true, which would be even worse than simply wondering. Plus, I'd feel terrible for having brought up the issue.

    I stood to leave and the sun returned. Maybe I had to visit this place one last time to say good-bye to Marie Harem, who may or may not have been related to me. At least I helped show her some kindness, versus dumping a cat on her doorstep.

Disinherited Son

Gloria Powers didn't want to board her dear cat, "Abby," not after something terrible happened: she left the "special food" for Abby at the check-in counter of tony "Bark and Purr Pet Resort" in Scottsdale, Arizona, while Abby was taken via her carrier, to the cat kennel area. The employee, "Crissa," returned with the carrier and handed it to Gloria. Since all the paperwork for boarding Abby was out of the way, Gloria took the carrier from her and indicated Abby's food was still on the counter. Gloria proceeded to take a four- day trip to visit her former college roommate and her family in Michigan, and upon her return to pick up Abby, the bag of special food was still sitting in the same place! Gloria started to blame herself for having absentmindedly held the bag of food while Crissa was looking in the carrier and cooing at Abby. (Gloria was very proud of the fact her cat was an extremely gorgeous, white short hair with green eyes.) Crissa had even asked if Abby had her own food, and Gloria had told her yes. Gloria hoped Crissa eventually lost her job over another, similar, indefensible error. She in fact wasn't there when Gloria picked up Abby, but that was supposedly because she wasn't due at work until noon that day. At the very least, Gloria had wanted to give the young woman a piece of her mind, but once Abby and she were back home, Gloria decided that would have been a waste of time. It was better to not patronize the place ever again. (She did remember to bring the bag of food back home with her.)

Gloria considered making use of the boarding facilities

Amy Kristoff

offered at the veterinary clinic where she took Abby, "Thunderbird Animal Clinic," but it was just a basic kennel, although its reasonable price reflected as much. Admittedly, Dr. Brad Cellus would undoubtedly make sure Abby had her special food because he was the one who prescribed it! The trip to Michigan had been the longest one Gloria had been on since acquiring Abby two years earlier, as a one- year-old. Gloria had taken a few overnight excursions, but she had left Abby at home. It hadn't been a perfect arrangement, but nothing bad had happened, although Gloria had made sure Abby was restricted as to where she could go.

Another four-day trip loomed, this time to Colorado to rendezvous with three classmates from high school (social media had allowed Gloria to reconnect with friends from her past like she never could have imagined). She also made more use of technology than someone like her son could have imagined. As a divorcee who would have also been a widow at this point, since her ex recently passed away, she was always looking for places to go and people to see. Although she looked forward to going away, Gloria did not want to board Abby, nor could she leave her alone in the house that long. In the past week she had interviewed three pet sitters, one over the phone and two in person, and none of them seemed promising. Gloria was sure one of them was first and foremost looking for a place to crash for a few days, even though she had a registered LLC for her pet sitting business. It would have been funny if Gloria wasn't so serious about the best possible care for her Abby!

***

It had been a slow morning here at Valley Bank on Hayden Road in Scottsdale, and Grant Powers was contemplating what to have for lunch just to keep himself busy. He had to do a wire transfer for a customer shortly after he got here at nine, and nothing much had happened since. Just as

Short Cat Tales

he was about to order some food online from "Augustino's" and have it delivered, versus walk half a block to pick it up, his phone rang. After saying, "Valley Bank, Grant speaking," his mother said, "Grant, it's me. I know I'm not supposed to call you at work unless it's urgent, but something is really bothering me."

The door to Grant's glass-sided office was closed, so he was technically at liberty to go off on his mother. Nonetheless, he would never do that because there was too much at stake. That was to say even though she divorced Grant's dad, Norman, back when Grant was in college, she was the sole heir to her ex-husband's money. What had initially appeared to be a "small-to-medium sum" had turned into much more. Grant wasn't sure if his father had recently updated his will, or that was how he had wanted his estate distributed all along. Either way, Grant accepted it, although it kind of bothered him to think he had technically been disinherited by his father – yet did he nothing wrong to deserve it. He wanted to make sure he remained in his mother's good graces, to help his chances of not being "doubly disinherited." He thanked his lucky stars he was an only child (and the reason for that was his birth was "difficult" for his mother).

Grant had his appetite taken away, thanks to his mother's phone call. Some would have said he was making too big of a deal out of doing his mother a favor, especially since he just declared it was imperative he remain on excellent terms with her. She was the epitome of a sweet, little old lady until she decided someone did her wrong. After that, the individual might as well be dead, no matter how trivial the issue.

The phone rang again, and this time it was Grant's girlfriend of three years, Lydia. She called him about every weekday before lunch, and they chatted for a couple minutes if he wasn't tied up with something. She worked at the Valley Bank on the corner of 68th and Camelback in Scottsdale, less than a block from where he lived, "Casa del Monte," a walled compound of tan brick and off-white stucco, two and three-bedroom condominiums.

Grant could barely return her greeting before launching into his complaint: "I have been told by my mom to take care of her cat for four days coming up because she's suddenly paranoid about boarding the thing, but she's determined to see the world as well as reconnect with every friend she's had since kindergarten, and the cat isn't her idea of a traveling companion."

"Wow, I guess you hate cats," Lydia remarked.

"Cleaning the litter box is what I am going to hate. Or picking up the crap if the cat goes someplace other than the litter box. I guess I could let my mom deal with it when she gets home from her trip, but I don't think she would be too happy about that. She's pretty meticulous despite having the cat and would expect me to step up."

"Grant, since I work right down the street, I can take care of the kitty both in the morning and after work. I was a tech at a vet clinic part-time for years and am very familiar with cats. My family never had one because my mom is allergic to them. I know you like to play nine holes of golf or go to the driving range after work, so once you need me to take care of the cat, give me your mom's house key, and I don't have to bother you for it if you're not around for whatever reason." Lydia knew Grant's mother's unit number and location because they had picked her up several times to take her out to dinner.

Grant was so grateful for Lydia's offer he wished he could have hugged and kissed her through the phone. His mom kept warning him Lydia was going to be the one who got away if he didn't propose, but they had a solid relationship by tacitly agreeing to keep things monogamous yet still having separate residences. She had never pushed him for more commitment than what they had, so unless she started hinting she wanted an engagement ring, he wasn't about to start shopping for one, nor was he going to ask her to move in with him. He figured that would be the arrangement since he

Short Cat Tales

owned his place, while she was renting an apartment. The only times she stayed over were on the weekends or holidays. She had almost too many interests and crammed as many activities into her free time as she could. He never feared she had another boyfriend because she was too busy.

Grant's two-bedroom, ranch-style, detached condominium was on the south side of Casa del Monte, the grass courtyard in the back the only bit of real estate between his unit and the ten feet high, tan brick wall and Camelback Road. His mother's two-story, three-bedroom unit was in the very middle of the compound, in a cluster of stucco units, all newer than the original brick ones, mostly one-story, that lined the entire perimeter. The streets were set up in a grid, so it was very easy to find each unit, no winding streets or hidden front entrances. The lap pool and outdoor sitting area were near her condominium, as well as a large covered patio, which was adjacent to the tan brick, flat-roofed building that had a conference room for the quarterly homeowner's association meetings as well as an office for the Casa del Monte property manager, Susanne Hall.

Before Grant started dating Lydia, he went to the weekly, Friday evening, happy hour get-togethers that took place poolside at Casa del Monte, from November until April. It was an opportunity for residents, both year-round and seasonal (snowbirds), to congregate. Grant attended first and foremost for the free food, although it wasn't technically "free," since the monthly homeowner's association fee helped pay for it. A second reason he went to these come-as-you-are shindigs was to hopefully meet someone, but a Valley Bank-related get-together was what put him in contact with Lydia, and he was immediately smitten.

Lydia had recently started working for the bank and was flying up though the ranks so quickly, the bank president, Cal Rose, threw the meet-and-greet/congratulatory dinner in her favor, at the "Cork 'n' Cleaver" in Phoenix. Anyone but Lydia would have become egomaniacal as a result, which made her all the more irresistible. Also, she had shown up alone, so there was no concern on Grant's part in regard to stepping on another man's toes, at least not for the evening. There were twenty-three at the table, only Grant, Lydia and Cal having arrived without a significant other. Debra Wansell was the manager of the Valley Bank in Glendale and was to Lydia's left. She'd brought her husband, Mike, and mostly talked to him or the couple across the table, Cathy and Nick Schein, the latter the manager at the Valley Bank in Fountain Hills, so Lydia was essentially forced to put up with Grant and seemed to enjoy that fate. Meeting her had not only been like a breath of fresh air, but she made him realize he'd been wasting his time with every past relationship and found himself thinking, So this is what love is like.

Grant ended up asking Lydia out to dinner the following Saturday, and he picked her up at her place, near Interstate 17, just north of Camelback Road. It was an iffy area in his opinion and told her so when she got in his car. She laughed and told him, "Since I'm now working at the Valley Bank at Sixty-eighth and Camelback, next weekend I'm moving closer to that location. Hayden and Verde Valley to be exact. My new place overlooks a huge park with plenty of places to walk and bicycle. I can't wait to get outside more."

Initially Grant feared if Lydia lived too close, she'd stop by all the time and wear out her welcome. However, that had yet to happen after three years, and he actually wished she would come by on a week night for a change and do nothing but sit around. He would be happy to skip playing golf or going to the driving range in the evening if she wanted to visit. (It was understood she would visit him, versus the other way around, since his place was more spacious and easier to access.) He was jealous of her busyness, as ridiculous as that sounded. No, he took that back. He was jealous, period. That was the best he could do to get mad at her. In fact, there was absolutely nothing unlikable about her. Grant's mother was right; he'd be a fool to let her get away.

Short Cat Tales

The problem was he was a fool.
    Gus and Sherman Maste were Lydia's two younger brothers, both extremely fit and capable of moving their sister's furniture and belongings to her new apartment, especially since each one drove a pickup truck. Upon Grant's insistence, he helped too, although his helpfulness was questionable in regard to the extent of it. First of all, he drove a newer, BMW 3 Series sedan and second of all, he was a comparative weakling. He was glad to find out she wasn't a hoarder, and he eyed everything in relation to how much of it would fit in his rather sparsely-furnished condo. Since his unit included the use of a two-vehicle carport, connected by a breezeway, there was no place to store any extra furniture. He was getting ahead of himself, but there was no denying his strong feelings for her. He even felt a little guilty for not taking a leap of faith and asking her to move in with him, but she certainly wasn't expecting as much, which made her all the more captivating.
    Grant hated to admit it, but he was sore Monday morning, following the moving event. The pain was mostly in his legs, as Lydia's new apartment was on the second floor, versus the ground floor like her former one. Also, there was a long, winding sidewalk that led from the parking area to her apartment building, and there were intermittent steps, since the building was on a hill, although at the Valley Bank where he worked on Hayden Road, the area was as flat as a pancake. He got his exercise from golfing and occasionally lifting weights, but he wasn't in the great shape he'd assumed he was. Lydia's brother Gus actually worked for a moving company for a couple years to help pay his college tuition. Both brothers were impressively strong, and Grant was relieved not to be in contention with them to win Lydia's heart, at least not in the romantic sense. They appeared to approve of Grant, and he tried to be as nice as possible. Anything to give him an extra point in Lydia's eyes!

Amy Kristoff

***

When Gloria asked Grant to take care of Abby while she was in Colorado, she had no idea the implication of it. First of all, since he had never owned a pet (his choice), it wasn't exactly a big surprise his enthusiasm level for the favor was zero. However, he was always a pretty straightforward individual, at least she'd thought so. Then this. To be more exact: upon Gloria's return, she looked over the video from her in-house cameras, and he didn't set foot in her place the whole time she was gone – his girlfriend, Lydia, did! All he'd had to do was tell his mother he intended to have Lydia take his place, but no. Gloria even called him at the midpoint of her trip (two days in), to ask how Abby was doing, and he had the gall to reply, "Fine!" Just like that! To think it never occurred to him, she might have a way to keep an eye on things and wasn't completely out of it in regard to technology.

Gloria wanted to think she raised a better son than appeared to be the case. Maybe she tended to make too big of a deal out of some things, but when it came to her Abby, honesty was extremely important.

The only thing Grant understood was money (he worked at a bank, after all), so she would make sure he was cut out of her will. It would be more worthwhile to leave everything to her cat.

The Cat Tale Pond

Buying a horse boarding stable was not unlike buying a residential rental property that already had tenants, meaning in both cases you had "instant cash flow." However, in regard to the house, you had to wait for the lease to end to get rid of the tenants or have a valid reason to evict them. As for the stable, you were in potentially murkier waters if things weren't working out with a boarder or his or her horse. Obviously if the boarder was behind on payments, there was legal recourse, but it was basically impossible to get rid of a boarder because you didn't like him or her. That was the case for Ava Land, the owner of "Happy Trails Boarding Stable," in St. Charles, Illinois. The boarder who really rubbed her the wrong way was Carrie Menten, the owner of a dark bay Dutch Warmblood gelding, "Ringo," (not named after the iconic Beatles drummer, Carrie liked to point out).

Overall, purchasing this five-acre property on Hunt Club Road was a dream come true for Ava, and she had lived here for only a few months. She couldn't have afforded to simply buy "horse property," not in this area. She had formerly owned a mobile tack shop and traveled to horse shows in several states, selling tack and equipment. After nearly twenty years of doing that, she had decided to sell her business (van included) and a small house in downtown St. Charles and try to find a manageably-sized boarding stable nearby (hers had twelve stalls). Luckily she knew of a capable real estate agent, Ivy Keating, who was able to find properties before they even came on the market. Ava's place was formerly named "J and M Stable," owned by Jan and Mike Sharkey, who moved to Florida. Ava named the property in relation to the Illinois Prairie Path, which was on the other side of the street, popular with bicyclists and joggers as much as equestrians. Because it was a very horse-friendly area, drivers were prepared to yield to riders who wanted to cross the road, although there were a couple boarders who still refused, so they were limited to riding in the indoor or outdoor ring or the open field behind the barn, which had a small pond (and getting smaller lately because it had been so dry). Fortunately there were old oak trees and plenty of vegetation, so it was very private, particularly in the summer months, as it currently was, mid-July. Also, all the surrounding properties were five acres if not more, so no one in the vicinity was crowded out by a subdivision.

Ava had moved into her new house alone, in the literal sense of the word. She was single and didn't even have a dog or a cat. Her last dog, a Jack Russell terrier mix rescue, "Punky," passed away two years ago and had traveled everywhere with her. Starting over with another dog was out of the question, so she proceeded to immerse herself in more work than ever. That was probably how she came around to the idea of owning and running a boarding stable: she knew the chores and responsibilities would never end, which was a peculiar kind of comfort.

As for a cat, Ava never had one live with her, but when she was growing up there were always some around the horse property her parents owned in nearby Bartlett. Her mother, Ruth, rode dressage, competitively at one point, and she encouraged Ava to ride too. It was a far cry from the typical horse-crazed girl who had to pester her parents for even one group riding lesson. Her parents weren't wealthy but were discriminatory with their spending. They ended up with more than enough to retire on after selling their ten-acre property to a developer. They too moved to Florida and

Short Cat Tales

although in their eighties, they were still able to live independently.

When Ava moved in to her new place, she found it noteworthy there wasn't a single cat roaming around, not even a raggedy-looking stray passing through. It was understandable if the Sharkeys had some barn cats they took with them, but one would have thought there'd still be a cat sighting of some sort. Ava decided one of the neighbors probably left a huge bowl of dry food on the porch, and all the cats, stray and otherwise, went there. They would also need some water, since accessibility to it was probably becoming an issue, given how little it had rained in the past month.

On the boarding agreement the Sharkeys had for J and M Stable, it was stated boarders could access the property "during regular business hours, seven days a week." Ava didn't especially mind having Happy Trails open every day, but regular business hours to her were eight to five. Ideally, no boarders would be allowed to visit their horses before noon every day, but that wasn't realistic. At least she'd gotten over the oppressive need to "stick around" every time a boarder showed up. At some point she intended to modify the boarding agreement, as she was currently using J and M Stable's (which the Sharkeys had drawn up by an attorney). If she wanted Happy Trails to be closed one day a week, it was her prerogative.

This particular day, a Tuesday, was supposed to be warm and muggy with a good chance of an afternoon thunderstorm. Ava didn't care for rain, let alone severe weather, but she was kind of looking forward to seeing some precipitation. Then, right after she'd finished cleaning the stalls, about eight-thirty, who showed up but Carrie Menten. Ava was headed to the house to have a bite to eat, but she felt obligated to wait and chat with Carrie, once she parked her white Lexus IS 500 and got out. After doing so she exclaimed, "Morning! Thought I'd beat the heat and see Ringo super-early today."

Ava nodded, saying, "Good morning to you, too. That's a great idea. Are you going to ride?"

"I might. I can take Ringo back to your pond and see if there are any dead cat bodies, since the water's got to be pretty low with this drought we're having."

"The what?"

"Dead cat bodies," Carrie repeated. "Mike positively hated cats, so if any dared set foot on the property, let alone go in the barn, he'd trap them and drown them in that old sewer pond you have."

All this "information" was becoming difficult for Ava to process, so she asked, "Exactly how do you know all this, including the one about the pond?"

"Educated guess, Ava," Carrie replied. "It was man-made, dug for a house that was torn down. As for the cats, I witnessed what Mike did, on more than one occasion. What bothered me the most was Jan didn't tell him not to do it, and she'd conveniently make herself scarce when it happened."

"They were both really helpful, giving me plenty of useful information about running a boarding business," Ava said, aware her remark was hardly a defense for the Sharkeys' possible attitude toward cats. Honestly, Ava didn't believe a word out of Carrie's mouth, but that comment could be saved for another day – when she'd had enough of the boarding horses lifestyle, which included the unwanted obligation of tolerating a lying windbag.

The Guard Cat

"The Little Store" in Wood Hollow, Indiana had been owned by Minnie Eisel for close to sixty years, and nothing "bad" had ever happened, other than a neighborhood kid occasionally sneaking some gum or a candy bar. Usually she caught him (rarely a girl) red-handed, and the item would be returned to its rightful place without incident. Otherwise, the culprit knew not to bother showing up at her store ever again. Wood Hollow didn't have a whole lot of businesses, so it was important to be respectful of the proprietors here who were willing to basically live on less. Although Lafayette was only about a half-hour due south, with its tremendous growth over the years, at least in part due to the large university in the area, visiting Wood Hollow was almost like taking a step back in time.

Located in a two-story, brown brick building at the corner of Main Street and Harrison Avenue, The Little Store not only offered candy, gum, and assorted snacks, there was a counter with half a dozen brown vinyl stools that swiveled, where patrons could sit and enjoy a cup of coffee, as well as a few breakfast and lunch items, all prepared by Minnie at the stove facing the diners. She didn't get rich doing this for a living, but she did manage to help pay her two sons' college tuitions. They also worked during the summers and school years. Widowed at nineteen, when one son, Terrence, was a little over a year old and the other, Lyndon, was a newborn, Minnie and her sons moved into the two-bedroom apartment above the store. Granted, if it hadn't been for her mother-in-law, Josephine, practically giving her the building and the business when her son (Minnie's husband, Seth), unexpectedly passed away, Minnie probably would have sunk into deep despair. She hated to take advantage of her mother-in-law's grief-stricken state, but Josephine insisted and made a point to show Minnie how to run the store. Coincidentally, the apartment was vacant at the time, which helped convince Minnie, moving into it was "meant to be," since it was usually occupied by tenants. With "Wood Hollow Park and Recreation Area" less than half a block away, her sons would have a place to play once they were older.

Living above the store was so convenient, Minnie never even considered moving, so once she was officially an empty-nester, it made more sense than ever to stay put. Some days climbing the stairs was a bit difficult, but it simply wasn't in her to complain or heaven forbid, retire. On cold winter days, there was definitely no better living arrangement. Helpfully she was a "cat person" versus a "dog person," so her feline companion didn't expect to be taken outside to do her (or his) business.

Minnie had one cat or another since childhood, and when she and her sons moved above the store, she had a fifteen-year-old orange tabby named Mandarin. Always a bit of a sourpuss, she underwent a personality change when she started following Minnie downstairs to work, six mornings a week. Kids loved to pet her, and she couldn't seem to get enough of the attention. After ascending the stairs at the end of the work day, Mandarin became her mopey self again.

After Mandarin, who made it to nineteen, Minnie had a black-and-white shorthair named Dahlia. She was adopted through "High Meadow Veterinary Clinic," where Minnie had taken all her cats for vaccinations since she married. It was therefore where Mandarin was taken once it was obvious she wasn't going to make it. The clinic was on the outskirts of Wood Hollow and had both a small and a large animal veterinarian on call. That was the one time Minnie went straight

Short Cat Tales

from owning one cat to another without at least a week in between. She didn't pick a female on purpose, but she did believe a female cat was the most suited for living indoors.

The last female cat Minnie had was Gabby, a light gray shorthair, who was given to her by the owner of Wood Hollow Hardware, Harry Lundquist. He retired at 77, and Gabby happened to be his store mascot. Harry's son Brett took over the business and was all business, so having a cat hanging around the store would never do. Harry's wife, Samantha, didn't care for cats, and it was too late in life to change her mind. Besides, her Havanese, Poppy, supposedly mercilessly harassed cats, so that would be the end of peace and quiet in the Lundquist home. Poppy needed to be put in his (or was it her?) place by a fed up cat, was all.

Anyway, Gabby made it to fifteen, dying in her sleep. Not long before her passing, her former owner, Harry, died too. Minnie had coincidentally started thinking about how she was getting up there in the years herself, so maybe it was time to not have a cat. In less than eight months, she was going to be eighty! If the next cat lived as long as the others had, it was very likely Minnie would pass away first.

Then, about three weeks before Thanksgiving, Minnie's only grandson, Caleb (his father was Lyndon, married to Paula, both professors at the nearby university), stopped by the store to say hi in the afternoon with his fiancée, Tracy, and Minnie served each of them a cup of coffee. Then she finished cleaning up before closing for the day, chatting while working. Caleb and Tracy seemed perfect for one another, having met at "Countryside Animal Hospital" in Delphi, where Caleb had recently started employment. He was in fact Dr. Caleb Eisel, DVM, and Tracy was an assistant manager and part-time groomer there, having started working at the clinic even before she had her driver's license!

Tracy's father, Mitch, was a cop, and her twin brother, Thad, was in training to become one. Minnie was very respectful of the profession, but she wondered if "the law enforcement background" of two close family members skewed Tracy's ability to be reasonable when she stated, "You can never be too careful any place you live these days, Grandma. You should have a plan in case you're ever here alone and some unsavory character shows up out of the blue and, well, basically ruins your day somehow."

Minnie just nodded, not wanting to plan for anything more involved than how many eggs she would need the following morning for the breakfast patrons. At the same time, Tracy was right. Pretty, petite, and rather short with long brunette hair she usually wore in a ponytail, the young woman had an impish demeanor that was easy to see would be beguiling to a man. She had dimples when she smiled, making her even more alluring. Caleb had mentioned going places with her and how she turned heads, despite her small stature. He joked, sometimes it seemed like she was from another planet because of her beauty and otherworldliness.

Caleb changed the subject by asking Minnie, "Grandma, are you getting another cat?"

"Actually, Caleb, I'm not sure. I was thinking of taking a 'forever' break." Then tears came to Minnie's eyes. Luckily her back was turned at that moment, as she was just getting done with cleaning the stove.

"You should have a companion, Grandma," Caleb insisted. "Ever considered a dog? One that is sure to bark would be perfect if some drunk comes around and bangs on the front door in the middle of the night. That's probably the worst that would ever happen around here."

"She needs a guard cat, since she prefers cats," Tracy said, sounding completely serious.

Minnie wanted to answer her by saying, "Yes!" but figured Tracy was having some fun with the cat dilemma. Therefore, she said, "If only they existed."

"Do you mind boy cats, Grandma?" Tracy asked. "One that's fixed, of course."

"No, not really, although for one reason or another I've

Short Cat Tales

always had a female. My mother had a male cat, Rascal, and he was really friendly, but I doubt if he was fixed."

Tracy said, "For a Thanksgiving present, Caleb and I are going to give you a cat. I guarantee you will love him." Then she winked at Caleb, who appeared as puzzled as his grandmother but nodded obediently.

Sure enough, Thanksgiving morning, before Minnie was slated to join Caleb, Tracy, and Caleb's parents for dinner at the latter's house in Lafayette, the young couple stopped by with a medium-sized pet carrier, which Tracy opened right inside the front doorway of The Little Store. An absolutely gorgeous solid orange cat emerged, not even remotely afraid or tentative.

"He's so big!" Minnie exclaimed. "But is he ever beautiful! What kind is he?"

"Maine Coon," Tracy replied. "His name is 'Tigger.' I recommend keeping that name because he's used to it."

"How old is he?" Minnie wanted to know.

"I believe he's five. I left all his papers in Caleb's truck, so I'll run back out and get everything."

Minnie wished she had enough time alone with Caleb to ask him what the heck was going on. As much as she appreciated being given a cat who appeared show-worthy, at least to the untrained eye, she didn't feel like she deserved him! Someone in Tracy's family must have owned his parents, and maybe he was supposed to be used for breeding too but things didn't work out.

In no time at all, Tigger became Minnie's buddy, and he followed her literally everywhere. At the same time, if she went outside, whether to take out the trash or leave for some errands, he never attempted to escape. She wasn't about to become complacent because of his size as well as the fact he was a little chubby; he could effortlessly slip past her and out an opened door if he wanted to. Minnie was grateful he chose to stick around.

Amy Kristoff

***

By February of the following year, Minnie and Tigger were closer than ever, and she relied on him for her incentive, especially on a cold, snowy morning. Groundhog Day just came and went, and the prediction was six more weeks of winter. It made Minnie start wondering if she shouldn't close up shop for a couple months a year, maybe longer, and go someplace warm. This wasn't the first time the thought occurred to her, but she finally felt the urge to save some extra money and make a plan for next year. She couldn't afford to splurge but could figure out an economical winter living arrangement.

The Little Store technically opened at eight, but Minnie started making breakfast preparations around seven-thirty and often times unlocked the front door at 7:50. On this particular morning, since it was so blustery out, she wondered if she shouldn't hold off on getting everything ready and plan on very little breakfast business. That meant she wouldn't unlock the front door until exactly eight o'clock. Larry Kern, who opened the hardware store for Brett on Wednesdays, at eight-thirty, occasionally stopped by for a quick cup of coffee first. However, the weather had to be decent, as he parked his truck behind the hardware store and walked a few doors down to The Little Store, before heading back to Wood Hollow Hardware. If Minnie had not yet unlocked the door when he showed up, he would usually bang on it since time was short for him—in more ways than one. He had to be pushing ninety. Minnie wasn't bothered by his show of impatience because he always left a good tip.

Just as Minnie was about to get out a couple mixing bowls and cooking utensils, someone loudly banged on the door. Right away, the hair on the back of Minnie's neck stood on end because that wasn't Larry. Whoever was outside wanted in, and although the weather was unpleasant, the temperature wasn't subzero.

Short Cat Tales

Minnie walked up to the door and stood on her tiptoes to peer through the diamond of glass at the top, finding herself eye-to-eye with a nearly bald-headed, grizzled-looking man who was probably in his forties but had a hardened facial appearance that made him look older. He definitely wasn't familiar. Feeling a strange compulsion to memorize the man's face, Minnie stared at him and couldn't seem to look away. He used the opportunity to say, "I'm from out of town, and my car broke down a couple miles out. The auto repair shop isn't open yet" ("Jerry's Quick Fix"). "I could use a cup of coffee and a place to warm up for a few."

Minnie sensed trouble but couldn't seem to get herself to listen to her inner voice! She was almost certain Jerry's was already open, as the owner was a workaholic and showed up about seven- thirty most mornings, even when the weather wasn't the greatest. Jerry always made sure there was fresh coffee brewing in the waiting room, and occasionally he stopped at "Erma's Bakery" on the way and picked up a couple dozen assorted doughnuts. Minnie wanted to tell the guy to go back to the repair shop, it had to be open, maybe it just didn't look like it. On a morning like this one, neither one of the two garage doors was open.

"The coffee's just started brewing, so there's a wait," Minnie said.

"Fine with me," the thug told her. "Like I said, I need to warm up, so could you please let me in?"

Since Minnie was politely asked to open the door, she felt obligated to do so. Nonetheless, her subconscious kept telling her otherwise. As if her hands and fingers were moving involuntarily, she proceeded to unlock the door and turn the knob. In the meantime, Tigger had been sitting, watching, at the bottom of the wooden stairway leading to the apartment. Barely was the door unlocked when the thug pushed on it and entered, nearly knocking Minnie flat on her back. Luckily she was able to keep her balance, no small feat given the suddenness of the assault as well as her rather slow reflexes.

The thug quickly locked the door again and appeared prepared to terrorize Minnie – or worse. She attempted to back away, with the intention of phoning for help, but he grabbed her left arm, twisted it and shoved her toward the register, to the left, telling her, "Scream and you die, and I'll start by breaking your arm."

The pain was so intense, Minnie couldn't help crying out, and from behind her, Tigger emitted a yowl that mimicked the sound of his owner's in volume! However, the difference was what came out of his mouth was noticeably more guttural, and it immediately got the thug's attention. And just as the hoodlum made eye contact with Tigger, the cat sprung forward and leaped onto his head, scratching it and covering his eyes with a wildly swinging tail. In no time Tigger made the thug so miserable he let go of Minnie's arm, yelling expletives. The cat then jumped off the hoodlum's head, but not before clawing him, and stood in front of Minnie, who was shaking and sobbing. The danger had passed, as the thug unlocked the door and departed, blood trickling down his face and the back of his head. He was still swearing but was mumbling the words, as if frustrated and maybe even embarrassed, he'd been had by a cat!

Trinket

Cindy and Bobby Mackley were finally allowed to have a pet. Although Cindy had wanted a cat, Bobby was adamant a dog was the best choice for a furry companion. Cindy, age nine, a year younger than her brother, happened to be obsessed with drawing cats, and although she was above average in talent, she was no prodigy. Therefore, her renderings of cats weren't exactly masterpieces, and Bobby mercilessly criticized them. If that wasn't bad enough, neither one of their parents, Debra and Len, ever made more than a feeble effort to deter Bobby from making his verbal attacks. Debra was all for letting both her kids "freely express themselves," so Bobby was entitled to say something negative, even in relation to his sister because it would never damage her morale. As for Len, he typically paid cursory attention to his two kids, and he'd admit to as much. However, he was always behind the scenes, so to speak, discussing family matters with Debra, so it wasn't as if he didn't care about them or was out of the loop.

Debra and Len had several lengthy discussions about whether their kids should have a dog or a cat, and one reason they kept talking about the issue was to buy time, meaning they hoped the kids forgot about even wanting a pet. That didn't happen, so they had a couple more discussions and made their conclusion. When their kiddos tired of the novelty of owning an animal, a cat was more likely to not only tolerate but be indifferent to his or her caretakers' indifference (whether the indifference was sudden or gradual).

Amy Kristoff

Another issue Debra and Len agreed on was they were not about to run out to a pet shop and buy a kitty, nor were they going to rush to the local animal shelter and immediately pluck a kitten from a limitless heap of kitten litters. The whole family would be "on the lookout" for a kitten (or even a cat if he or she wasn't too old), and it would be a purposely deliberate (time-consuming) process.

Coincidentally, Debra and Len enjoyed going to garage and yard sales, and they typically turned the outings into family affairs, often heading to subdivisions south of their house in Spring Glen, Indiana, where it was more rural. In turn, the offerings at these garage sales included more "countryish" items, such as a used tractor or a garden tiller. They thought it was important for their kids to realize you could buy something inexpensive and used, and it could give you as much pleasure or provide as much use as something brand new, although it might require effort to get it to that point.

"Prairie Rose" subdivision on the outskirts of Pleasant Hill, in the west-central part of the state, had a garage sale every June, on the first Saturday the kids were off of school for the summer. It was worth the forty- minute drive due south on the interstate just to look at the houses, all of which appeared to be at least three-thousand square feet, on three to five-acre lots. The land was as flat as a pancake, so the name of the town couldn't have been inspired by where this subdivision was located.

Cindy and Bobby were silent in the back seat of the Chevy Tahoe for the duration of the trip, although they had a spat right before departure, regarding a cat being the pet they were allowed to get. Bobby was determined that decision was reached to keep Cindy from throwing a temper tantrum, and he was being taken for granted (he would never throw a tantrum to get his way). Their parents were aware of the gist of the argument, but neither one bothered to chime in and clarify matters. In turn, they figured the silence between

Short Cat Tales

their two kids was "a good sign." Debra and Len could never have been accused of disagreeing about how to raise them.

Having arrived at the entrance to Prairie Rose at almost eleven, there was unanimous amazement at all the vehicles parked on either side of Honeysuckle Drive, which snaked around to other streets. Debra liked the subdivision because it was in a rural area yet had curbs and sidewalks. She'd told Len more than once, "If we ever save enough money and something we like at Prairie Rose comes up for sale, we're moving!" Their cozy tri-level in Spring Glen (in "Hope Manor" subdivision) more than adequately met their needs, and Len wouldn't be thrilled with the extra commute time. He worked over the state line, in Illinois, at "Pets, Inc.," a pet supply distribution center. There was an allure to getting away from what had become a rather crowded area, thanks to many residents moving to Spring Glen and other nearby towns from none other than Illinois.

Len ended up parking at the very corner of Honeysuckle Drive, on the right hand side, wedging the Tahoe into a space. Instead of starting the bargain hunting at the house on the same side of the street, a two-story with brown cedar siding and a three-car garage with two dormers above it, the Mackleys crossed the street to investigate what was offered for sale at a white vinyl-sided, two-story house with a wrap-around porch and a large garage just behind it. All four doors were open, three of which had a vehicle in the space, including a newer white Corvette, a matching yellow one, and a new white Chevy Suburban. There were a few large items in the one space there wasn't a vehicle, but they may not have even been for sale. The Mackleys never got past the first long, folding table that was closest to the house, on top of which there were various used household tools and appliances and under which there was a large metal crate, inside of which was a wicker basket with a plaid blanket, making a bed for six gray shorthair kittens! Cindy noticed them first and "squealed like a pig," Bobby would later say. At the time he just rolled his eyes and wanted to go back and sit in the Tahoe. Debra and Len realized the cause of Cindy's excitement and were almost disappointed. At the very least they wanted to walk around the neighborhood awhile, visiting some garage/yard sales that looked particularly interesting, but Cindy would undoubtedly be determined every kitten would be adopted in the meantime.

No one appeared to be around, to ask about the kittens, so Len suggested they visit some other houses and could return shortly. Debra volunteered to stay with Cindy, and they could wait for the homeowner to appear. Len and Bobby could go ahead and look around.

Finally the homeowner, Emma Steiner, emerged from the side door. A thin, rather frail-looking woman with wispy blonde hair, she greeted Debra and Cindy with a cordial hello, and they did the same. Emma then said, "My son is the one who set all this up and he was supposed to be here to handle everything, but he took off on his motorcycle! My husband got a ride to the golf course to play a round of golf so he's gone for sure. Every year I say I'm going to lock up and be out of town when this neighborhood sale comes up, but somehow, I'm always here."

"We were interested in one of your kittens," Debra said.

"Good!" Emma said and told Debra her name, so she did the same and told her Cindy was her daughter.

"Could I look at them?" Cindy asked, hardly able to contain her excitement.

"Certainly," Emma answered. "You and your mom, go ahead and pull the crate out from under the table. I was trying to keep the kittens shaded, but they have that water bottle in the corner if need be."

"How old are they?" Debra asked while she and Cindy moved the crate.

"Eight weeks and a day," Emma replied.

"Is that all?" Debra wanted to know.

"That's just old enough to be weaned, but they do need

their first round of vaccinations. Since I haven't had that done yet, anyone who takes a kitten this weekend gets him or her for free."

Cindy looked over all of the kittens before choosing one. Debra slowly opened the crate door, and Cindy carefully reached in for the kitten, one that was slightly darker gray in color than the rest. He didn't mind being taken away from his siblings, and Cindy held him in her arms. Meanwhile, Debra closed the crate door, and Emma looked closely at the kitten Cindy had chosen, saying, "That's a male, in case you were wondering."

"Is that O.K. with you?" Debra asked her daughter.

"Yes, except I wanted to name whatever cat we got, 'Trinket.'"

"That can be a tom cat's name, why not," Emma remarked.

Debra nodded in agreement and added, "The kitty won't know the difference."

That was indeed the case, but as soon as the Mackley family was back on the interstate, with Trinket in Cindy's lap, a tan cotton throw, "free" from Emma, providing a bed for him, Bobby let loose on the taunts about how stupid a name that was, let alone for a "boy" cat.

Cindy found it almost impossible to ignore him and wondered why her parents didn't tell him to shut up. Finally she said, "He's your cat too, so you name him."

"I dunno what to call him and don't care. I wanted a dog."

Debra said, "We have zero supplies for Trinket, so we're going to stop at the strip mall at exit sixty, and I'll run in and get some things at the pet shop there. Hopefully it's still in business."

"I just won't call the cat anything. There," Bobby quietly said, making sure only Cindy heard him. Maybe their mom missed his comment about the dog. It was possible she was simply ignoring him. He might not get his dog until he turned eighteen and left home, which he intended to do. It was a

Amy Kristoff

long way away, so he felt comfortable making a threat like that.

While Debra was in the store (it was an independently-owned establishment called "Pets and Aquatics Galore" and carried some Pets, Inc. products), Len and the kids waited in the Tahoe, the engine running and the air-conditioning on because Cindy was worried about Trinket getting too warm. Bobby couldn't resist telling her she squealed like a pig when she first laid eyes on the kittens under the table in the driveway. Afterward he proceeded to push up the end of his nose and lean toward her, making an oinking sound. Len somehow managed to notice what was going on, and while looking back at Bobby via the rearview mirror, told him, "Stop it. Now."

Bobby nodded but almost couldn't help himself, especially since he had gotten by with his antics for so long. Now he had an added target: a stupid kitten named Trinket. This was going to be fun!

Don't Let the Cat Out!

Staci Millner was having a hard time finding the right house for a particularly discerning buyer of hers, Mike (she would forgo his last name to protect his privacy). As a broker associate at "City and Country Real Estate" in Chelmsford, Indiana for close to a dozen years, she considered herself to be very good at finding the right house for every client she worked with. Occasionally it took a little longer than she expected, but she had yet to fail to pull it off. With Mike, however, it was possibly going to be a first, if only because of low inventory. Since she hadn't made Mike sign an exclusive agency agreement, he was free to leave her in the lurch, so to speak, if he tired of having her show him houses. In other words, he could fire her before she had been allowed to do her job. More than once over the years (probably half a dozen times, easily), she had contemplated quitting real estate, thanks to situations similar to the one she was in. Circumstances beyond her control managed to make her appear incapable, and it was extremely humiliating. Granted, that attitude was a bit over-the-top, but she took any setbacks to heart. Real estate wasn't simply a career for Staci; it was a lifestyle. When she wasn't taking clients to listing appointments, she tirelessly went to open houses, both ones for buyers and broker-only ones. She also enjoyed visiting model homes featured at new developments and made some beneficial connections that way. Although she was occasionally a listing agent for a property, more often than

Amy Kristoff

not she referred a potential listing to another broker associate in the office. She was allowed to accept a referral fee but in turn wasn't bothered with all the headaches of being the listing agent.

Anyway, all this was to say Staci had become very adept at deciphering what a property was really like, not simply from the marketing remarks at the top of the listing or the accompanying photographs, but the agent remarks. She liked to think she could in fact determine whether a property was worth looking at from the agent remarks alone. There was one she held off making an appointment to show to Mike because in the agent remarks was the following: "Don't let the cat out!" Staci's first thought was, Duh! Her second thought was, Mike would never want a house, any house, no matter how nice it was or meticulous the sellers were, that had a cat as a "former resident." He was a fastidious bachelor who traveled extensively for his travel blog, and when he was home, he wanted plenty of space, inside and out, although he lived alone and had no pets.

Therefore, because of the cat, Staci assumed it was a waste of time for Mike to go through 7437 Lankin Lane, in unincorporated Chelmsford. Nonetheless, the property met many of his requirements. The house was spacious at 3,000 square feet; the lot was generous in size as well, with 1.5 acres; and the price was relatively reasonable at $399,999. All the nines in the price irritated Staci more than the innocent cat. The house had been on the market for close to a hundred days, so it was time for something to give, as in perhaps there was a small price reduction? If there was, someone would most likely snap it up. Staci was headed to the office and could look up the listing to see if the price had dropped. From the pictures she'd viewed previously, it was an atheistically-pleasing house, resembling a two-story A-frame one would find on a farm. It was built in the 1990s and appeared to need some interior updating. That wasn't a deterrent to Mike if the original materials were above-average

Short Cat Tales

and the house was structurally sound. Still and all, everything came back to the cat, and it would have to remain hidden during the showing. Then again, there was inevitably a food or water bowl to contend with, as well as a bed of some sort—unless of course the cat slept with its owners. That possibility was enough to make Staci nauseous. She'd never want a cat to begin with, but if she did, it would never share her bed!

Just as Staci pulled into the parking lot of the strip mall where City and Country Real Estate's office was located, she had an "Aha!" moment, realizing she ought to preview 7437 Lankin Lane! It was only a few miles from the office, but even if it was a bit of a drive, she wondered why she didn't consider doing so sooner? She could scope out the cat situation and decide how much its presence was a detriment to a showing. Also, she could confirm if the cat did any damage that would require replacing wooden window frames or trim, as well as the condition of the flooring, some of which was wood. She was certain Mike wouldn't be satisfied hiding any stains with throw rugs and would instead have the entire floor refinished. She was assuming as much about him but had to be right, especially since he didn't have any pets.

The office was pretty quiet for a Monday at almost noon. The receptionist, Lacy, took long lunch breaks in order to go home and take care of an ailing family member, so she was already gone but did have calls forwarded to her cell phone unless an agent cared to take her place until one or one-thirty. That was what Staci did, the day Mike happened to call the office and was very gregarious. He was also specific about what kind of property he was interested in and emailed a recent mortgage pre-approval letter to her after they spoke. He was a dream client before they'd even met!

There were three large computers available for use, each one in a spacious cubicle with an L-shaped Formica desk, allowing seating for as many as six people. In fact, there was an agent going through some listings at one of the computers, which was by the window overlooking the parking lot, and Staci could see the top of five heads besides the agent's. She was the only Realtor in here, it appeared. The managing broker, Alice Barrone, often times didn't show up on Mondays until mid-afternoon, especially if she'd hosted an open house the day before. City and Country Real Estate employed about a dozen agents, so even if Staci saw the woman's face, it was possible she didn't know her. Also, some of the agents worked almost entirely remotely and hardly ever showed up at the office. Anyway, Staci logged on to the computer closest to the receptionist's desk and looked up 7437 Lankin Lane. The price had in fact dropped, to $390,500, so there would probably be more showings and possibly a contract on it soon. One golden rule she recalled from real estate school was "Time is of the Essence," so what she really needed to do was go ahead and find out when Mike would be available to look at the property, skipping the preview after all. She'd been lucky thus far, showing him properties between his work-related trips, not having to wait a week or more for his return. She'd call him before making the appointment request online, but she'd first check to see if something new was on the market that might be of interest to him as well.

***

Mike didn't want to let down the Realtor, Staci, who had been showing him properties in or near Chelmsford, Indiana, but he was starting to have a change of heart about buying a house at the present time. It was nothing personal, but he had a feeling she would never believe him. He happened to have an aunt who was a Realtor (in another state) who told him it was imperative to have "a thick skin" to survive as an agent, although Staci had anything but that. Supposedly she had been in real estate for ten years or more and seemed to know her stuff but was super-sensitive.

Short Cat Tales

At this point, Mike was traveling so much for his internet-related business, he would rather keep hitting the road than bother with the responsibility of home ownership, having originally planned on settling down a little. Lately his trips were practically free, and he was also paid to write articles about the destinations, which were used for advertising purposes by the paying parties and were also posted on his website (for which he received reimbursement). This was exactly the place he'd been working toward ever since starting his blog three years ago. Having left the corporate financial world behind to be his own boss, it was not the time to slow down! His one-bedroom apartment would do just fine for awhile longer. Besides, after a year or two, maybe there would be more housing inventory, as there wasn't a whole lot to choose from, especially since he preferred to remain in or near Chelmsford. Rather than live in a cookie-cutter subdivision with barely any yard, he'd told Staci he wanted at least an acre of land to go with a 2,500 or even 3,000 square foot house. Aware a property such as that meant the house most likely was not new construction, he was willing to do some updating/remodeling but had no desire to gut the entire interior, even if was a steal.

What Mike wanted to purchase appeared to only exist in his mind because Staci had shown him probably eight or nine properties by this time, stretched out over a couple months, and none of them checked all the boxes (and there weren't many boxes that needed checking). At least two houses practically needed gutting, yet the prices hardly reflected as much.

Since Mike was willing to bet money Staci would have a meltdown over the phone if he told her he wanted to take a hiatus from looking at properties, he would let her show him one or two more and then tell her face-to-face afterward, he was going to temporarily put his house-buying venture on hold. If she was a true professional, accepting his decision wouldn't be an issue. He'd even promise to contact her (ver-

Amy Kristoff

sus another Realtor) when he was ready to start looking for a property again. In the meantime, she usually found a property or two for him to look at about every other week, so she was due to contact him soon. That would be great because he was leaving for Thailand next week; he could get the showings (and her) out of the way prior to his departure. It wasn't his intention to sound callous; it was simply a matter of business being business.

***

Staci couldn't find any properties besides the one on Lankin Lane to show Mike for the time being, so she called him and briefly described it before suggesting they meet there the following day if he was available at one o'clock. He sounded happy to hear from her and readily agreed to that time. She reminded him she still had to request the appointment and have it confirmed before it was a go. He said he was able to look at it later than one if necessary or even the following day. In fact, he was pretty much available until next Monday, when he was going abroad. Staci was so focused on showing the Lankin Lane property, it never occurred to her to ask him where he was jetting off to next! The last thing she wanted to do was be rude! She happened to mention she'd hesitated recommending he see the property because there was a cat and she "just knew" he didn't like cats—or any animals, most likely, given his on-the-go lifestyle. The daily care of a pet had to be his worst nightmare. There was complete silence on Mike's end after Staci made that last remark, and she ended up asking if he was still there. He said yes and then told her he'd see her at 7437 Lankin Lane the following day at one, unless he heard otherwise. She told him she'd email him the listing so he could look it over in the meantime. He thanked her and that was the end of the call.

***

Short Cat Tales

Mike coincidentally just got off the phone with none other than Staci the Realtor, and she had a property to show him tomorrow. It sounded like it was pretty close to what he'd been looking for, but since he had a change of plans, he wouldn't be making an offer. There was no chance of letting Staci down because she would be happy to be rid of him when he was done griping about all the real and/or imagined cat smells, etc.

"Isn't that right, Felix," Mike said to the fourteen-karat gold urn he removed from the top of his bedroom dresser. In it was stored the ashes of his beloved Siamese cat, Felix. "There can never be a replacement for you, even though I keep renting this apartment specifically because they do allow cats and I pay extra for it. You went too soon, way too soon. Maybe I'll finish grieving someday. Ha! If only that Realtor lady knew!"

One Crazy Former Cat Owner

Ana Caruthers always wanted to go into business for herself, if only to avoid boredom, which was what she felt when a boss told her what to do, day in and day out. Obviously it wasn't the fault of the higher-up. Also, Ana was self-motivated and in turn frustrated when her self-motivation wasn't put to use. Some individuals started businesses to make lots of money and become wealthy, but for Ana it was all about her frame of mind. Plus, she wanted an opportunity to spend more time with her Dachshund, Tino. If she worked for herself, she could make her own rules about having a dog in a work environment, whatever it might consist of.

As luck would have it (for Ana), her best friend since sixth grade, Deirdre Clarion, went through a divorce after twenty-five years of marriage and received a generous settlement, along with a mortgage-free house in Cave Creek, Arizona. As a divorcee and empty-nester, Deirdre wanted to start a business too, and like Ana, she wasn't out to make millions. She just wanted to stay busy and earn some income while she was at it. Because she was at the ready with the necessary financial backing, Ana was eager to make a plan with her.

The two friends put their ideas together and came up with starting a closet organizing business. Here in the Phoenix valley, plenty of residents had the means to concern themselves about such matters. Not only that, they had plenty of superfluous possessions that were in need of organizing (versus selling or tossing out). In some cases, "superfluous" was an understatement. Ana was in charge of the measuring, designing, and layout of the closet organization set-ups, as well as providing a physical location for the business, on her five-acre, former horse property. Deirdre took care of fielding inquiries via phone and email, and she was in charge of ordering the materials, balancing the books, and scheduling the installations. Deirdre's former brother-in-law, Tim, handled the installations. As a licensed contractor, he provided the necessary expertise and was able to offer valuable input on the projects. After all, what good were shelf units and storage compartments that were hung or placed improperly? Tim happened to think the world of Deirdre—in a brotherly way—so having him on board was yet another piece of the business puzzle that fit perfectly.

Ana enjoyed visiting potential customers' homes whenever she was contacted to assess their closet organizing needs and present an estimate. At times she felt like a voyeur because yes, she took everything in, at each house she visited. She always expected the inhabitants to make sure their houses were tidier throughout than they typically were, including the multi-million dollar ones. Maybe it was human nature to let a house be a bit messy if the estimator for "That's One Organized Closet!" was stopping by. Or more appropriately it was a cry for help!

Going on five years already, Deirdre and Ana (and Tim) had been running a successful company. It was turning a respectable profit, and word of mouth appeared to provide the most reliable source of advertising (and it was free, no less).

Some residences, Ana had returned to more than once, in order to organize a different closet. She knew TOOC (the abbreviation of the business's name) was doing something right, to be called on to organize more than one closet at the same house. Since she usually only saw part of a house when she was invited inside to look at a particular closet and write up an estimate, it was like visiting a new place. One

Amy Kristoff

homeowner in Paradise Valley had a large walk-in closet in the main bedroom organized recently and said she wanted Ana to organize all the closets in the three-bedroom guest house. Ana couldn't wait to see how large and resplendent the guest house probably was, given the size and opulence of the main house (sixty-five hundred square feet, white stucco, French chateau design).

Tim's remodeling business had picked up thanks to the superior workmanship he did for TOOC. Conversely, TOOC was often contacted to provide its services in conjunction with a remodeling project of Tim's. Lately, however, business was slow, but that was expected. The middle of July was when summer homes were visited, either in the northern part of the state or in another part of the country. Ana only had one appointment today, at ten o'clock this morning, at a residence that was only a couple of miles from TOOC's office (the converted twelve by twenty-foot tack room of the four-stall steel barn behind her house in North Scottsdale). It had air-conditioning, a water cooler, and three metal desks, although Ana used hers far more than Deirdre and Tim used theirs. Those two did a lot of their work from their respective homes, and Tim's wife, Patty, helped him run his remodeling business from there as well.

The barn aisleway and stalls provided plenty of storage space for all the materials needed for the various closet organizing projects. Having owned horses when Ana resided on the property with her parents, Rick and Emma, doing so once they moved out and she moved back in was financially impossible. They had sold her the place at a bargain-basement price, as the white brick, ranch-style house needed a lot of updating (and still did). Ana's father had a number of health concerns, and it was convenient living in a townhouse close to the medical facility in Mesa where he was being treated on an outpatient basis. He and his wife had wanted to downsize for years anyway and knew Ana missed the property where she grew up. In the meantime she had lived in various apartments while trying to find a job she loved. It was enjoyable to finally have some space again, and acquiring Tino had been an indulgence, having not owned a dog since high school. With a successful business as well, Ana felt like she was onto something. It was better late than never!

The address of Ana's one and only stop this morning was 5012 Wagon Wheel Way, about a mile and three quarters north on Scottsdale Road and then east on Wagon Wheel, at the end of the long cul-de-sac. All of the houses on the street were tan, brown, or terra cotta-colored adobe-style, on one acre lots that were natural desert in the front and sides, to meet the subdivision requirements. The ones on the north side abutted state-owned land, which included the tan adobe house that was 5012. Ana turned into the circular driveway, which consisted of the packed desert, and parked her white Kia Sorento beneath the shade of a large mesquite tree. The only two places there was any concrete was under a huge, white canvas awning, where a brand-new-looking motor home was parked and a small area in front of the three-car garage, which was discreetly placed perpendicular to the front of the house. Thick, tan adobe walls surrounded the front entry area, and it was necessary to open a tall, black wrought iron gate to reach it. Not until Ana was in this area did she see any noticeably-sized windows, which were on either side of the rustic wood front door with a hammered copper overlay. All the other windows in front were very small and recessed, with cross panes.

Since the brown wooden shutters on the windows on either side of the front door were closed, it was impossible to see any movement inside once Ana knocked on the door. Typically she showed up for her appointments and didn't call or text first. She in fact left her phone in her vehicle and only had grid paper, a pen and a tape measure with her. Almost a minute passed before she heard a woman's voice from inside say, "I'm coming! I'm coming!"

Ana wanted to tell the woman, whom she assumed was

Amy Kristoff

Darla Connor, not to hurry, she had all day. In the shade here it was still livable, but you could tell it was going to be very hot by midday.

Ms. Connor opened the door and offered a hearty hello, and Ana identified herself while handing the homeowner a business card. Ana was five foot -five and Ms. Connor was shorter than herself. Typically for these appointments, Ana wore white pants and a short-sleeved, white cotton shirt with the company name in black script on the front, her first name in block letters below. She was proud of TOOC and wanted her appearance to reflect as much. Ms. Connor was wearing pale pink pedal pushers and a white short-sleeved shirt with pale pink polka-dots. Even her slip-on sandals were pale pink. She must have been spending some time outside because her face and arms were deeply tanned. She had to be seventy or more but had few wrinkles. If she had cosmetic work done, she still looked human.

"Would you care for something to drink?" Ms. Connor asked.

"No, thanks, I'm fine," Ana replied. "If you want to show me the closet you have in mind to redo, I can get some measurements and have an estimate for you in no time."

"I hope not! I was expecting you to sit down with me for at least a few minutes. My husband Frank still works all day, and we don't even need the money. I lost my beloved cat, Esmerelda, just a month ago, and I feel completely lost and alone. That motor home out there was what I drove to the cat shows and pageants with her. She was really special, and she's the reason I called you. I have dozens and dozens of outfits and costumes I bought for her over the years, and I would like to look at them from time to time but not remove them from the closet to do so. With both Frank and I with kids and grandkids from our previous marriages, we have a revolving door of houseguests, and they like to make fun of me with my collection of kitty outfits I keep hidden. I was thinking of having something installed like the rack drycleaners have for customers' garments. The closet I have in mind should be able to accommodate one of those. That'll show them."

After Ana extended her condolences to Ms. Connor about her cat, she said, "The shelf and rack set-ups I have available won't be movable like that, but it will be possible to display the outfits. Tim the installer is really imaginative and always has an idea or two to add to mine yet keep things within a budget."

"That's good! Otherwise my husband will have an excuse to keep working for another ten years if I spend too much on this project. He doesn't even like vacations. It was no small feat to get him to travel with Esmerelda and me a couple times before she passed away."

While Ana followed Ms. Connor to the closet in question, she thought about how she never had the same conversation twice in this business, for sure!

Ms. Connor led the way through the living room, which had a Saltillo-tiled floor and large cross-beams above. A large rug that appeared to be made of burlap was on the floor in front of an overstuffed, mustard-yellow, L-shaped leather sofa, over which a brass ceiling fan was whirling away. The sofa faced the side of the room where there was a large, whitewashed, ceiling-high console, which appeared to be an elaborate entertainment center. On the wall to the left of the sofa there was a watercolor painting in a thick, wood frame and was easily four feet by four feet, consisting of the head-shot of an orange tabby. It was cartoonish in nature, and the background was very colorful, with swirls of purple, blue and green. It was unique and eye-catching but at the same time garish. With the thick adobe walls and sparseness of décor, this part of the house seemed like it could have doubled as a sanatorium, not that Ana had ever visited one.

Once the hallway leading to "Esmerelda's room" was reached, the picture situation changed dramatically. On both walls there were countless five-by-seven and eight-by-ten-

Amy Kristoff

inch professional, color photographs of whom appeared to be Ms. Connor posing with a cat, not all the same cat, definitely not an orange tabby in many of them, assuming that described Esmerelda. Ana only had a few seconds to take everything in, as she didn't want to appear nosy. Then again, perhaps Ms. Connor would have been flattered. Ana was curious to know exactly what a cat competed in, besides "Best Dressed." There were in fact several in which the cat in the picture was wearing a costume of some sort. Evidently Ms. Connor attended many a cat show and/or pageant, possibly well before she traveled to them in a sumptuous motor home.

Ms. Connor entered the second room on the left, which had an oak floor and more pictures but not photographs of her and a cat. Some were framed cat posters, and others appeared to be pictures removed from cat-themed calendars. The windowless room was about twenty-by-twenty, and there were pictures literally everywhere on the walls. There was a small brass pet bed in a corner, but there was no cushion of any sort, just the frame. Also, there was a white wicker basket beside it, containing some cat toys. The only wall that wasn't overloaded with pictures was where the closet was located, behind a ceiling-high bi-fold door.

Before opening the closet door, Ms. Connor said, "The room we are now in, was originally supposed to be a walk-in closet. There is a guest suite on the other side, and I decided it was too generous of a space for someone who wasn't supposed to be living here full-time. As I'd mentioned, we have practically non-stop guests as it is, thanks to our respective families, and I prefer to display all the cat outfits and costumes than keep everything hidden. Besides, I can't look at them the way they are now." Then the bi-fold door was opened and out spilled some of the "dozens and dozens" of cat outfits and costumes in question. The thing was, it looked more like there were literally hundreds and hundreds. They were stuffed on a single, narrow shelf, as the closet had practically no depth.

Ana looked around the room that was supposed to have been a closet and declared, "That automatic rack you were referring to, might be your best bet after all, provided you're interested in giving up most of this space for it. Tim would be the one to do the measuring and estimating for the project, since it wouldn't be something we normally install. He would also have to run the electric for it, so that would have to figure in the total cost."

"There goes my budget," Ms. Connor said. "I'll think about it and get back to you. I really ought to go through all the costumes and outfits and throw some away. At the same time, I'm afraid I won't be able to part with a single one, even if I try! As lonely and heartbroken as I am, I doubt I ever have another cat, which gives me even less excuse to keep all these around. Or maybe that gives me the best reason of all, I don't know."

Ana ended up leaving Ms. Connor's without any expectation of hearing from her. Nonetheless, it didn't feel like a completely wasted day because it was so enjoyable meeting new people, including ones who obsessively collected cat clothes.

One Lying Cat Owner

Mr. Norm Thomas had been renting an apartment in a three-unit from Mr. Jared Gottlieb for several years and always paid the $850 on the first of the month, in person. He'd walk about a third of a mile to "J.G.'s Gas and Mini Mart" at the corner of Roderick and Main in Greenbriar, Indiana to do so. The owner was none other than Mr. Gottlieb, who was usually manning the register. It wasn't a very big place, just four pumps, no diesel, and if the mart itself was busy, it felt really crowded. Anyway, if Mr. Gottlieb wasn't front and center at the register, his wife, Maryl, was and would take the rent money (all cash, in a blank, letter-size security envelope) and tell Norm, "I'll make sure my husband gets this." In response, Norm would nod, nothing more. He in fact gave her the rent money last month. Mr. Gottlieb's Buick Century wasn't parked in the back like it usually was, so perhaps he had dropped her off and left to run errands. Sometimes he was simply in the office inside the mart, hence he was nearby. Even though Maryl appeared to be a bit younger than Norm (he was pushing fifty), she was definitely a lot younger than her husband. It might have been her first marriage, but it wasn't Mr. Gottlieb's. Norm knew this because one of the units in the converted two and a half-story A-frame where his apartment was, was rented by a son of Mr. Gottlieb's. His name was Jesse, and he was a trash pick-up driver. His mother, Holly, stopped by once a week to bring him containers and sometimes plates of homemade meals. Like Norm, Jesse was single, lived alone, and never

Short Cat Tales

had any visitors (besides his mother). Norm wondered how the guy managed, although his job probably helped keep him mentally occupied, and his mother's meals helped him, too. Norm worked from home and rarely left. He collected medical bill payments over the phone, which was, at times, depressing work. Although he actually sided more with the poor schmo who couldn't pay the amount due, a job was a job, and Norm liked to think he was pretty good at his. He wasn't lonely, not only because he was a loner but he had constant companionship, in the form of his cat, Fiona. The problem was, he wasn't supposed to have a pet. It stated as much in the lease he'd initially signed. At the time, Norm had justified having a cat because the rent seemed exorbitant, especially since he had to hand over a $850 security deposit, too. However, since Mr. Gottlieb never raised the rent, it no longer seemed so bad, and Norm even felt a little guilty. One reason he could so easily keep up the deception was the fact Mr. Gottlieb had never once requested doing a walk-though of the unit. Norm wasn't a slob and was pretty strict with Fiona, but absent the cat, it was still rather obvious there was a longtime feline resident. The third tenant was an older lady, Glenda, who worked at "Violet's," the florist shop in town. (Violet happened to be the first name of the owner.) Glenda knew about Fiona, but she would never tell on Norm. At least, he didn't think so.

    The monthly walk to pay the rent was the most exercise Norm got every thirty days. On this particular first mid-morning of November, the wind was brisk, and as Norm made his way to "J.G.'s," he was cursing the fact he hadn't dressed more warmly. He tried to get angry about it, just to help warm himself up, but it didn't do any good. He decided instead to think about the cup of coffee he intended to enjoy once he was back in his apartment.

    The gas station was dead, as in there wasn't a single vehicle being fueled up, nor was there anyone inside the mart, at least no one who drove here. However, Mr. Gottlieb's

Amy Kristoff

Buick Century was in its place, in one of the spaces behind the building. Norm didn't know what Maryl drove; she didn't work at the gas station full time and got a ride from her husband when she did. Norm had no idea where the Gottliebs lived, but he bet their house was swankier than their vehicle(s).

Norm liked when there was no one here at J.G.'s because he could walk right in the mart, hand over the envelope with the rent and be on his way in seconds flat, offering no more than his signature nod of acknowledgment, no matter which Gottlieb was present. It was like a silent, seamless effort and beat the heck out of waiting behind customers mulling over what lottery tickets they wanted to purchase. As it was, he considered lottery tickets to be a pointless indulgence and was proud of his unwillingness to succumb to the temptation to purchase some too. He had his budget for living expenses (and for Fiona's care) down to the last penny and would never dare "splurge."

Once inside the mart, it indeed appeared to be void of people, other than Mr. Gottlieb, staring at some papers on the counter. The second he looked up and saw Norm, he grabbed the papers and started waving them, exclaiming, "Your rent money last month helped fund these @%*#& divorce papers!"

Norm innocently stated, "Maryl told me she'd make sure—"

"She's a liar! Or was a liar. Good riddance to the lying you know what. The bad part is I gotta 'divide the assets,' so she's gonna get half, the lazy you know what. I'll buy her out on the rentals, she ain't gonna get half of those. She wouldn't know what to do with 'em, anyway."

Hearing that, Norm was never so happy to go home to loyal, reliable Fiona. Also, it sounded like Mr. Gottlieb intended to remain a landlord for years to come. Hopefully he continued to avoid doing a walk-through. Norm wouldn't mind if the rent went up, a little anyway, the price for being

Short Cat Tales

sort of a liar too, one thing he had in common with Mrs. Gottlieb.

Here, Kitty, Kitty

    Margot Sherman had a favorite place she liked to take her notebook and write poems on a nice weekend afternoon during the school year, which would be ending in another month. It was a wooden park bench overlooking a pond, with a wide, sloping, grassy area in between. The bench was within easy walking distance from her condominium at McCormick Ranch, in Scottsdale, Arizona. There was no source of any shade, so maybe that made it an unpopular place to sit, giving Margot the opportunity to write there whenever she pleased, even if the sun was beating down. She had not yet published any of her work and liked to think she was perfecting her craft. When she was ready, she would type all of the poems on her computer, send them to an independent publisher that appreciated her version of creativity, and eventually she'd have enough financial success to write poetry full-time. She considered herself realistic and undemanding; therefore this "plan" would "pan out." In the meantime, she would continue teaching art class to first through fifth-graders at a private, non-parochial school here in town. It was the teaching job of a lifetime, given the low stress-level and generous salary. Margot had a friend she met her sophomore year in college to thank for the big break, or she probably would have returned to her roots in the Midwest and wouldn't have bothered to search for a teaching position. The starting salary would have been too paltry to make it worthwhile, either here in Arizona or back in Indiana. She didn't need a lot to live on, but she was definitely accustomed to living quite comfortably.

Having grown up in a broken home (Margot's mother, Amalia, left her in the care of her, Amalia's, estranged husband, Keil, when Margot was in sixth grade), Margot always felt like an outsider. In the small Indiana town in which she grew up, it was a big deal to not have two parents, and she let their separation and divorce affect her because of that alone. When she was permitted to apply to colleges, Arizona State was her first and only choice, as she hoped to become a different person "out West," if only because of the different climate. That didn't happen, but after returning home for the Christmas break her freshman year, she found she had no choice but to permanently move out of the house. Her father had "become serious" with someone Margot couldn't stand to be around. That said, it wasn't as if Margot had a preconceived notion about the woman, Allyson. Maybe her father was attracted to women like Margot's mother and her future stepmother, both of whom were extremely self-possessed. It didn't help, Margot was the polar opposite.

Margot always had a feeling her father paid her way through college to make sure she completed her studies without any excuses not to do so. Later, if she came begging for financial assistance, he could tell her he helped her all he could. Therefore, he essentially invested in his own peace of mind, which was understandable. At the same time, it seemed like he was relieved to be "done" with her, which fueled her feeling of being unmoored, a sentiment that never went away.

It was no surprise Margot's family never had a pet of any sort, even (or especially) when her mother was still around. Neither parent had any pets themselves when they were younger, so they had no inclination to at least give pet ownership a try. Lately Margot had been considering adopting a dog or cat, since she had been lonely and bored. She had zero inclination to date, which was helped by the fact her

Amy Kristoff

limited number of intimate relationships were dead-ends. A couple friends she made in college, Lisa and Shannon, were busy with their own lives (both were married and had young kids), and they never had the option to do something spontaneous, which kind of made Margot jealous! Owning a pet would give her a responsibility too, so she would have to make a schedule around a being other than herself.

With school winding down for the year, making it an especially favorable time to adopt a pet, why not a cat? She already did some research on them, as well as dogs, and it seemed as if a cat would be a good choice for a first-time pet owner like herself.

Margot reached "her" bench, and someone wearing a wide-brimmed, khaki-colored fabric hat, whose face she couldn't see, was seated there! She was so angry it was almost impossible to remain calm. Anyone who only knew her as the quiet, unassuming kids' art teacher, would have been shocked by the evil thoughts going through her head! Even she was surprised. Living alone as well as being "alone with her thoughts" evidently had a negative effect on her.

Notebook in hand, Margot took a walk on the concrete path, due north, where it passed behind a restaurant, "Nantucket's," that was accessed via Doubletree Boulevard, which ran east and west. Nantucket's offered both indoor and al fresco dining, and there was even a floating bar on the lower level. It had a nautical theme, with pylons supporting the outdoor dining part of the restaurant, and between the pylons there were two rows of thick rope for a barrier. There was also rope on either side of the wooden walkway leading to the floating bar.

Still and all, Nantucket's was a restaurant, and passing it where she did, Margot saw where the dumpster was located, surrounded by a concrete block wall on three sides and a tall, chain-link gate on the fourth. Just as she was almost past the enclosure, a white cat with azure blue eyes leaped from atop the wall, landing no more than a couple feet from her! Apparently he/she hadn't seen Margot because he/she looked as surprised as Margot was! As the cat took off toward the pond, Margot couldn't resist calling, "Here, kitty, kitty," holding out her free hand, hoping to at least touch that beautiful fur!

There was an especially steep slope between the walkway and the pond in this particular area, consisting of gravel as well as some large rocks (versus mowed grass, such as where "Margot's bench" was located). There was even a red metal sign that read "Danger" in white letters, while any other posted signs by the pond read "No Fishing or Swimming."

Between the loose gravel making traction difficult and Margot's choice of footwear (leather-soled flip-flops), she didn't stand a chance of keeping her balance while descending the slope. It appeared the cat had somehow gone under the walkway leading to the floating bar and disappeared. Margot actually considered trying to crawl under there! Falling down as she descended the slope was inevitable, so that was what she did, her notebook flying out in front of her and landing several feet away, in the pond. She was so upset about losing her "creative pride and joy," of which there was no copy, it took her several seconds to realize both her flip-flops had fallen off her feet, her left ankle was broken, and her elbows were severely skinned. She was a pitiful sight laying there, staring at her soggy notebook, too far out of reach to ever be reclaimed.

Tammy the Social Scaredy-Cat

Third-grader Tammy Senell walked to her friend Katie's house on Willowbrook Street to see the kittens after school one day. It was a couple weeks past Labor Day, and there was still summer weather, which helped make the walk enjoyable. Katie and her parents lived less than a mile from George Heller Elementary School, while Tammy and her family lived "outside the Lowell, Indiana town limits," necessitating a bus ride unless Tammy's mom was available to give her a ride. Katie's mom, Tina, was usually home, as she was on this particular afternoon. She offered Tammy something to drink upon the girls' arrival, and although Tammy was in fact thirsty, she was so eager to see (and hopefully hold and touch) the kittens, she didn't care about quenching her thirst! Nonetheless, she thanked Mrs. Tomlinson for the offer.

While Tammy and Katie sat on the tan carpeted floor in the living room, petting the five kittens, Mrs. Tomlinson watched, stone-faced, saying, "This will not happen again."

Tammy so enjoyed petting the kittens and spending a few minutes with them, she didn't want to stop! However, it was plain Mrs. Tomlinson was ready to drive her home, which was "the deal" since Tammy was allowed to miss the bus so she could walk home with Katie. This was like a trial run, since Tammy had never been deemed old enough to do this. In the future Tammy hoped Katie could ride the bus home with her, and then Katie's mom could pick her up after an hour or two. It seemed like Tammy's mom would be O.K. with that because she wouldn't have to take Katie home. The problem was Tammy didn't have a cute litter of kittens at her house! It was a pretty boring place but didn't have to be, with almost an acre of land on a traffic-free road. In fact, it seemed like it was "further out" than it actually was. Tammy's mom kept saying she wanted to convert an old shed behind the house into a coop and have chickens running around the yard and fresh eggs every day. Tammy's father said he lived on a road just like theirs, growing up in Illinois. He and his brother, Tammy's uncle Sean, took in animals people dumped in front of their house—mostly cats but one time two pet rabbits, both snow white. Tammy thought that sounded wonderful.

As much as Tammy wanted to stay on the floor with the kittens for a couple more minutes, Katie got up first and said, "My mom has to drop something off at my aunt Cheryl's, so we have to take you home. Maybe next time you can stay longer."

Tammy nodded at Katie and stood too, and she then glanced at Mrs. Tomlinson, who appeared relieved. It wasn't Tammy's imagination, Katie was told to say what she did, instead of her mother saying it. Tammy's mother couldn't pick her up this afternoon because she was at work as an in-home healthcare provider. Many of her patients lived even further from town than the Senells did, so the house calls often involved some driving, which sometimes lengthened her work day. Tammy's father, Brian, recently started a job "out of state," which Tammy's mom said she would explain "in more detail" at some point. All Tammy knew for sure was her mother hadn't worked for as long as she could remember and only started back up once Tammy's dad decided to leave "for work." Tammy didn't ever question her mom or any adults for that matter, but she was starting to think maybe she should. It was a lot to ask of Tammy to have to go home to an empty house some afternoons, although her mother promised to be home by four-thirty, "no matter what."

Amy Kristoff

Tammy and Katie knew one another since first grade, when they sat side-by-side in Mrs. Smith's homeroom. They didn't have the same homeroom teacher in second grade but did again this year, Mrs. Baker. Since they sat together, Tammy took extra notice of the fact Katie was not at her desk the next day and felt left out of not knowing the reason why. Katie might not have considered Tammy her best friend and vice versa, but she was definitely Tammy's only friend. Katie was the one who had initiated their friendship, or they might never have even become acquainted, thanks to how shy Tammy was.

When Katie's mother had driven Tammy home, Katie sat next to Tammy in the back seat of her mother's Ford Escape and had appeared noticeably glum, barely saying good-bye once Tammy got out. Tammy said bye to Katie and thanked Mrs. Tomlinson for the ride. Tammy was glad she hadn't bothered to add something about seeing Katie at school the following day because it would have been wishful thinking. Katie's absence made Tammy realize how valuable their friendship was to her.

It was impossible to pay attention to Mrs. Baker once the school day started because Tammy was distracted, anticipating having to sit alone in the cafeteria. She and Katie sat at the end of a long table near the entrance, with a space between them and about ten fourth and fifth-graders, including Jody Casten, who appeared to be the head of the group, despite being a new student. Her voice really carried, and she sounded like a know-it-all who seemed older than her years. Tammy was so discreet she was practically invisible, which someone like Jody probably could not relate to.

Typically Tammy had a sack lunch, so she didn't have to stand in line with a tray. Her mother prepared it, and she'd write Tammy's name on the bag so she could leave it in a specified place in Mrs. Baker's homeroom, along with the other students', often including Katie's as well. Sometimes, however, Katie bought a school lunch and would "warn"

Short Cat Tales

Tammy of as much, first thing in the morning. That way Tammy would know ahead of time she'd have to wait at the cafeteria table alone while Katie was standing in line. It was way better when they both had sack lunches, so they could dig right in together.

The group led by Jody Casten all had school lunches every day thus far, which made sense. Tammy couldn't imagine a single one of them with a mother who would bother to make them a sack lunch, not that any of them would appreciate as much. Occasionally Tammy's mom stuck a short note inside her lunch bag, saying, "I love you!" or "Have a nice day!" If only those girls knew, they'd have a good laugh!

Tammy felt as if she slept through the first half of the day, but she nonetheless worked up an appetite and was eager to eat lunch once her class was dismissed. She recalled her mother saying she put a piece of homemade fudge in her bag, for dessert. Her mother hadn't cooked or baked much of anything ever since Tammy's dad left to work out of state, so maybe she was finally adjusting, which was a relief. He was the one who said there was no reason to have a dog or a cat because "everyone was always gone all day," which wasn't true until recently, so he had simply been making an excuse. If he stayed away long enough, maybe Tammy's mom would reconsider having a pet. Then Tammy could remind her, Katie Tomlinson and her family had five kittens and would maybe part with one. Tammy never did find out what happened to the kittens' mother, if they still had her. The whole issue with the cats seemed to be really touchy, at least for Mrs. Tomlinson. Maybe Tammy could even offer to pay for a kitten, provided her own mother gave the O.K. (and lent Tammy some money if her allowance savings didn't cover the cost).

In the cafeteria, Tammy sat at her usual place, and she couldn't help noticing Jody Casten wasn't with her group. They already had their trays of food and were hungrily eating. Tammy decided to concentrate on eating her own food and minding her business. Right after she removed a small zip-lock bag of potato chips from her sack lunch and started munching on them, Jody yelled, "Boo!" right behind her. Tammy nearly dropped the bag with the potato chips, yet Jody howled in jubilation as if the entire contents of Tammy's sack lunch had just spilled all over the floor. That made Tammy madder than Jody's failed attempt to "scare her."

    Luckily, the group Jody had tried to impress was more interested in continuing to eat lunch than reacting to her attempt at a lame practical joke, so she stomped back to her place at the far end of the table. Tammy was proud of herself for basically ignoring Jody. She couldn't wait to tell Katie about this "mental victory" over the bully, Jody Casten. Maybe there was hope for Tammy yet.

The Cat Becomes Family

Conroy Glass was under a lot of pressure, some of which was self-induced because pleasing his mother, Alice, was very important to him. She wanted him to not only propose to his girlfriend of eighteen months, Gina, but marry her at the same time Conroy's older by a year brother, Zach, married his fiancée, Eileen. Those two put their wedding plans on hold while waiting for Conroy. They were amenable to whatever day he and Gina had in mind. Their willingness to be so patient and flexible put the entire onus on Conroy, which was very unnerving!

The biggest issue didn't involve Gina herself but her cat, "Miu-Miu." As much as Conroy wanted to tolerate living with the animal "'til death do us part," that sounded like too much to ask. Gina finally agreed not to let the cat share the bed with them, but Conroy still wasn't satisfied with the whole situation, although he kept as much to himself, for the most part. As it was, he did not want to marry Gina so he could turn around and divorce her, just to make his mother's day.

All that said, Conroy still felt an intense obligation to help make his mother happy, whatever it took. Her husband, Phil, Conroy and Zach's father, passed away unexpectedly almost three years ago, and she was absolutely devastated. The suddenness of his passing seemed to cause added grief, besides what she felt from physically losing him. Nonetheless, she tried to put on a brave face, yet Conroy knew she was often crying inside. She stayed busy with charity work as well as frequent lunches out with friends, but she lived alone. The

Amy Kristoff

Glass family never did have any pets, and Conroy's mother still wasn't interested in any canine or feline companionship.

An argument in Conroy's favor as to why he couldn't marry Gina was he didn't value pet ownership like she did because it didn't run in his family. Therefore, it was asking too much for him to ever really accept her cat. Not to defend himself, but he really did love Gina or the cat would have already been the dealbreaker (he wouldn't have invited her [and the cat] to move in with him after six months of dating). The bottom line was he couldn't be expected to propose, given the fact he was raised in a family that never had a pet, unless owning a large aquarium with exotic fish, counted.

In spite of no pets in the household growing up, Conroy had an ongoing affinity for dogs and wished Gina had one of those, instead. He thought it was fascinating, people walking their dogs, and doing so seemed like a great excuse to get out of the house, especially after a heated argument. In the Arcadia section of Phoenix, Arizona, where he lived, there was an abundance of quiet streets on which to enjoy a walk. Gina and he in fact had quite a few arguments, inevitably about that infernal cat of hers. Fortunately Conroy managed to keep his distance from the cat and vice versa. If nothing else, at least the cat wasn't dumb.

Conroy was a broker at "B.I.G. Real Estate" (Julian Bertrand, Mike Illone, and Conroy Glass), a commercial real estate company, and Zach was the attorney who the brokers called when needing legal services. Getting established in law wasn't easy, so he appreciated the business. Zach met Eileen through his practice, as she had been hired as a paralegal by the founder of the company, Russ Tannen. As for Conroy, he met Gina at his dentist's office, as she replaced "Trudy," the dental hygienist who had taken maternity leave. For Conroy's first cleaning with Gina, she was very flirtatious, and Conroy could hardly resist her charms, especially since there was no escaping her.

Conroy's mother's birthday was tomorrow, so he'd invited

Short Cat Tales

her to lunch. He'd asked Zach to join them, but he had a meeting at his office, he was required to attend. Since it would be just Conroy, he decided the thing to do was confess to her exactly why he couldn't propose to Gina. He couldn't imagine his mother failing to sympathize with his plight, but at the same time he didn't want to do any assuming. He would point out there was more to a wedding than the reception, cake, and keepsake photographs. After all the celebrating, Conroy would be legally bound to a woman with a cat. He was the first to admit it sounded silly to place a cat at the front and center of a new marriage, but the cat was most certainly at the front and center of this dilemma of his!

Conroy's million dollar question to himself was, what difference did it make to live with Gina and the cat, versus marry her? His answer was how the relationship would end: if they continued to live together and he finally had his fill, the worst that would happen when he told Gina to take her cat and leave was, she would make a lot of noise (and maybe the cat would, too). The end of their marriage would require an attorney, but that didn't mean Conroy could count on any discount legal services from his brother. Zach mostly worked on real estate issues, although he probably drew up his own pre-nuptial agreement to marry Eileen. Even if Conroy had one of those, he wouldn't feel any better about marrying Gina! He told her all the time he loved her, and she said it too, but did he really? Did she (love him)?

Was it possible Conroy didn't sufficiently love his mother and that was the real issue? He was mortified by the mere thought! It was fortunate Zach had no desire to "compete" with Conroy to be the most adoring son, or the latter would have gone crazy, trying to keep up appearances.

Here was a novel idea for Conroy: he would ask Zach what to do. The two of them weren't close, and that was actually a good thing in this case. Zach could maintain more objectivity about Conroy's situation because of as much and in turn supply him with some advice. Conroy could at least weigh what his brother said against his own thoughts on the "marriage matter."

Conroy was sitting in his office at B.I.G., too distracted to get anything done, so he decided to call Zach. He was probably at work too, so Conroy called his office and the receptionist, Mandy, answered, "Tannen, Corrales, and Glass, how may I help you?"

"Hi, Mandy, this is Conroy. Is my brother available?"

"No, he isn't. He's in a meeting. Can I take a message?"

"I thought his meeting was tomorrow at lunchtime!"

"He probably has one then, too. Should I tell him to call you when he's done?"

"I guess. It's nothing urgent, really. I was hoping to catch him when he happened to have a minute."

"I'll give him the number you're calling on, all right?"

"That's fine. Thanks," Conroy said and hung up, disgusted—not at any one thing or person, just disgusted. He wished nothing more than to have the same devil-may-care attitude as Zach—or that was how he seemed, compared to himself.

***

Zach just found out his brother, Conroy, called the office and wanted to chat—but it was nothing urgent. That could only mean he wanted to talk about the pointless alarm their mother had raised by assuming her two sons were all gung-ho to have a double wedding in her honor or some such nonsense. Conroy was a relatively successful commercial real estate broker, but he acted like a five-year-old when it came to their mother and pleasing her. Hell, she acted like a five-year-old too, anymore, making unrealistic demands of everyone. It started when she lost her husband to a sudden illness, and she realized the sympathy train never needed to stop. In other words, you were expected to cater to her every whim because she was a grieving widow—going on three

Short Cat Tales

years. Zach didn't buy into it, but Conroy sure did and could never tell her no, which was only spoiling her more and more.

What Zach wanted to do was tell Conroy to stand his effing ground, and if he didn't want to marry his girlfriend, don't! He'd wait a couple days and call him, however. Right now Zach was involved in some legal work he was asked to do with the other two attorneys at the firm. It was the moment in his career when things were really taking off. The last thing on his mind lately was getting married, not that his fiancée needed to know as much, but Conroy might appreciate the insight.

***

Conroy was at "The Lunch Basket" on Shea Boulevard at noon the following day, awaiting his mother's arrival. He was sipping an iced tea to quench his thirst, as it was a pretty hot day, typical of mid-May. What he really wanted was a stiff drink to calm his nerves, so his voice wouldn't quiver when he told his mother why he couldn't marry Gina. As an aside (but technically it was a valid point), her cat wet on Conroy's side of the bed last night, right before he laid down! He was able to pull the blanket off the bed before the urine soaked through the sheets and the mattress, but the whole event was disgusting. That was his opinion of course because Gina thought it was funny. He almost threw the blanket at her face, he was so angry. He told her she owed him a blanket, and that remark didn't go over very well. At least she shut up. The cat was supposed to be barred from the bedroom if it wouldn't stay off the bed, but Gina mistakenly thought it "knew" not to get on it. Conroy wondered how he could have given the cat enough credit to say it wasn't dumb. Then again, it was just plain sneaky, which did in fact require at least some intelligence.

Amy Kristoff

Conroy liked The Lunch Basket because everyone who worked here acted as if they knew him. Granted, a lot of the employees were not the same ones from when he frequented it, but they seemed familiar! The décor was casual, as it was a lunch/early dinner place, given the hours it was open. The food was absolutely delicious, whether it was the main dishes, the side orders, or the desserts. His mother was accustomed to dining out quite often, but she claimed not to have eaten here before. He was looking forward to her opinion, expecting it to be positive.

Since it was his mother's birthday, Conroy considered requesting the staff sing "Happy Birthday" to her after lunch, but she might not appreciate the gesture. She was pretty easygoing overall, but ever since her husband passed away, it was impossible to predict her reaction to a surprise, no matter how well-intentioned it might be.

Conroy had asked to sit near the entrance, which in this case meant his table was right by one of the three sets of double French doors that opened onto a flagstone patio with a small fountain. He wanted to make sure he could see his mother approach from the parking lot and enter via the main door. She could see well enough to drive, but in a darker area of the restaurant, she might overlook him. There were ceiling fans whirling overhead here, but it was undoubtedly cooler, further inside. He'd already warned the hostess, he might have to move to another table upon his mother's arrival. Since it wasn't yet too busy, his request wasn't a problem.

Then Conroy spotted his mother approaching the entrance. She was pretty hard to miss, dressed in white culottes, a white, short-sleeved blouse, and white espadrilles. In no time at all she was at his table, greeting him as he stood and they embraced. He wished her Happy Birthday and she thanked him.

Rather than sit back down, Conroy started walking toward the interior of the restaurant, suggesting to his mother it would be more comfortable there.

Short Cat Tales

She remarked, "It's fine right here. I like the open-air setting for a change."

"You're sure you won't get too warm? Now's the time to move, before it gets busy and we don't have a choice."

As his mother started to pull out a white rattan chair, Conroy hurried to assist her, saying, "I don't want you to get sick. You keep saying the heat doesn't agree with you."

"If I can't take it and no other tables are available, we'll just get up and leave, how's that?" she replied.

Conroy couldn't tell if she was serious or making a joke, so he just nodded. Then he sat back down.

The waitress, Rachel, appeared with the menus, and she asked Conroy's mother if she wanted something to drink. Conroy about fell off his chair when she replied, "I think I'll have a gin and tonic."

"Any specific brand of gin?" Rachel next asked, making Conroy sit up even straighter, were that possible!

"No, not really."

Conroy openly stared at his mother, trying to figure out what in the heck was going on with her, as she was not a hard liquor drinker, definitely not at lunch. Maybe it was a new habit of hers. Conroy couldn't understand why he was so upset, except for the fact he was surprised. It also didn't help, he had a craving for an alcoholic beverage, himself!

After Rachel departed with the drink order (including another iced tea), Conroy couldn't help asking his mother, "Are you a midday drinker now, Mom, or are you celebrating your special day?"

"It sounded refreshing to have a gin and tonic. Your dad and I used to have one after doubles tennis at the Merkners' on Saturday afternoons. That was before you were even born. Betty and Sid lived right across Invergordon. Their kids were already grown, and they ended up moving to Dallas to be close to their grandkids. Anyway, Betty's drinks were so tasty! Maybe I'm nostalgic because it's my birthday and I don't really want the drink at all."

Amy Kristoff

The gin and tonic and iced tea soon arrived, and Rachel asked if Conroy and his mother were ready to order or needed more time. Although Conroy's mother had barely looked at the menu, she claimed to know what she wanted. Conroy knew what he wanted before he got here, assuming the menu hadn't changed.

Conroy's mother ordered the grilled lemon butter chicken tenders and cream of broccoli soup. Conroy ordered the double stuffed meatloaf, finally looking at the menu to confirm it was still available. While his eyes were averted, his mother must have taken a swallow of her drink because she began loudly coughing. Barely one second later, Conroy leaped out of his seat and stood behind her, wondering if she was about to choke. She managed to set the drink glass back down on the table but continued to cough. One way or another, he felt destined to let his mother down, and since he didn't know how to execute the Heimlich maneuver, it was possible this was "The End"! He already felt guilty and selfish for not yet marrying Gina!

***

Alice had tears of happiness in her eyes as she watched her sons, Zach and Conroy, dancing with Eileen and Gina, their respective new brides. The ballroom at the legendary "Mountain Shadows" had been reserved for the wedding reception, and the wedding itself had taken place less than a mile away, in the backyard of Alice's property on Invergordon. Covering almost two acres, there was plenty of room to accommodate all the guests. She had wanted to have the reception there as well, but Zach wisely told her it was better to "have the party-part someplace else." She always trusted his judgment and appreciated his pragmatism. It was no wonder he was becoming an outstanding lawyer.

Conroy was much more emotion-driven than his brother, and Alice didn't want to exploit Conroy's nauseating solicitousness, but she couldn't seem to help herself. At her birthday luncheon a few months ago, she feigned choking on a gin and tonic she had barely sipped, and he was scared out of his wits! After that, nothing seemed insurmountable to him, including proposing to and marrying Gina!

As much as Alice wanted to tell both Conroy and Zach (and their new spouses) what she "faked doing" to bring the four of them together, it was probably better to keep it to herself—forever.

The Cat Writer

The printed announcement in one of the windows of "The Reader's Nook" in Scottsdale, Arizona, stated: "This Saturday from Noon to Two! Meet children's book author Deandra Gris! Pick up a copy of her latest Theo the Cat adventure, 'Mousing on Ramshackle Farm'! Have it signed! See you right here!"

Deandra actually saw this sign yesterday, Thursday, when she happened to be walking in the area where the book store was located, amongst the popular Fifth Avenue Shops. Deandra drove to that section of town to walk a couple mornings a week. She lived just north of 96th Street and Cactus in "Casas Grandes" subdivision, so it was only a few miles away. She got tired of taking walks around it, as it consisted of unvarying white stucco monstrosities with red tile roofs, including her own. Nonetheless, the house served its purpose: everyone who visited her was impressed, even her mother, Lena. She, by the way, was the one person who declared Deandra would never make it as a writer (let alone as anything else, for that matter). It never occurred to her mother it was possible to become a bestselling children's book author, which wasn't as easy as it sounded.

Deandra drew rough sketches to accompany her stories, although she wasn't obligated to do so, and they were forwarded to the illustrator, a very talented artist by the name of Clem Burrow. Deandra had yet to meet Clem face-to-face, but she never failed to show appreciation for his beautiful artwork by mentioning him in the Acknowledgment at the end of each of her three "Theo the Cat" books. She wanted to dedicate a book to him at this point, but her publisher, "Day Star Press," who had enlisted his services for her books, wouldn't let her! If she ever did meet Clem, maybe she could at least take him to lunch.

The book signing at The Reader's Nook was scheduled because the owner, Amber Knowles, had requested it, having seen Deandra shopping in her store numerous times. Deandra was flattered to have been asked and even more flattered to have been "recognized." Even though Deandra was a resident of Scottsdale, she had hardly ever done a book signing anywhere in the area! She never stopped and thought about that until this invite from Amber, which had to be "approved" by Deandra's publisher. That had initially irritated Deandra when she found out. Thanks to Theo the Cat, however, Deandra had signed all three titles of her books about an irascible cat, in bookstores in all fifty states! She also had the representatives of Day Star Press to thank for giving her the opportunity to make appearances all over the country, but it seemed unfair to need their permission to do a book signing locally.

One activity Deandra appeared to endlessly partake in was walking, as she was walking again this morning, this time where she lived. The book signing was tomorrow, and she was honestly kind of nervous. What if no one came? That would be an absolute embarrassment. Not only that, the owner of The Reader's Nook would be very upset because undoubtedly she wanted Deandra present, to help sell some books! Deandra wished there was a way to guarantee as much. She thought of the saying regarding publicity and how there was no such thing as the negative kind, but she did not agree. At least the time slot for the signing was only two hours. She'd been lucky thus far, none of her young fans had ever asked her any questions. In fact she was the one who would ask, "What is your first name?" in order to personalize a brief message she would include with her signature. Things

Amy Kristoff

could get dicey if she was ever asked something like, "How many cats do you have?" The truth would be impossible to reveal, yet she wasn't one to lie! It was bad enough she was starting to feel like a fraud.

As Deandra continued walking past the houses in her neighborhood, it occurred to her she didn't know any residents other than the families that lived on either side of her house, on Mockingbird Way. Even they were merely acquaintances. Having lived here for almost four years, it proved she kept to herself. None of them probably had any idea she was a "famous" writer.

The funny thing was, Deandra was never really into cats, yet she could write about one like she was. Her familiarity with them dated back to when she was growing up in Ohio, where her family had a couple acres in Forestville, a suburb of Cincinnati. Her mother or sister, Cara, took care of any pets they had, and all Deandra ever concerned herself with was getting good grades and eventually relocating to someplace where it wasn't humid in the summer. A vacation to the desert Southwest with her family one spring break in high school, made her more determined than ever to escape the Midwest. If it hadn't been for her writing success, she probably would have been stuck suffering through summers in or near her hometown for the rest of her life. The only thing the area she came from was good for, was providing a background for her Theo the Cat stories.

All of Deandra's family had remained in the vicinity of where she grew up, although every time Cara visited Deandra, she talked about moving. Retired from the airline industry, as well as divorced and an empty nester (her only son, Chad, worked for a non-profit and often traveled abroad), she was about as free as anyone could expect to be, yet her latest excuse for staying put was to take care of their mother. She purposely neglected taking care of herself since becoming a widow half a decade ago and was almost proud of as much. Nevertheless, she found the time to regularly criticize Deandra, which Deandra could not understand, until coming to the conclusion perhaps her mother was jealous. Even if that wasn't the case, it made Deandra feel better. Since Cara felt an obligation to "be there" for their mother, Deandra was glad because she sure as heck didn't! Deandra still invited her mother to visit for a week every year, and her mother managed to be on maybe not her best behavior but was still much less critical than she could otherwise be. Deandra most likely had her big, impressive house to thank. That notion brought her back to her original issue, which seemed to be gaining momentum in her head: she was nothing but a fraud. Something would have to be done about it.

***

Deandra arrived at The Reader's Nook at 11:50 Saturday morning, and the first thing she saw upon entering was a stack of easily thirty copies of "Mousing on Ramshackle Farm"! Her stomach fluttered, as she considered the very real possibility, every single copy might end up returned to the publisher at the end of the day. That was how disgusted Ms. Knowles would be when not one Theo the Cat fan, showed up. And realistically, any young reader was as interested in the main character of a book as much or more so than he or she was in the author.

Having shopped in The Reader's Nook countless times, Deandra knew where the book signing table was, so she made a beeline for it, passing a couple of customers, including one who was with a light blonde-haired girl of about seven, just the right age for a Theo the Cat book. She was with an older woman, possibly her grandmother, who was browsing in the Cooking section. Maybe they were waiting for the book signing to start.

Ms. Knowles intercepted Deandra about halfway to the table, welcoming her and asking if she would like something to drink. Deandra said she'd brought a bottle of cold water and left it in her car, so she went back out to retrieve it.

Upon her return, Deandra noticed a young boy waiting at the table. She hurried to her place and was glad to see a couple pens were already laid out. She said hello to the young reader and noticed he had all three of the Theo the Cat books. He explained his mom helped him purchase the first two online and the most recent one, "Mousing on Ramshackle Farm," he was buying today with allowance money he'd saved. He wanted to know if Deandra could please sign all three?

Nodding, Deandra said, "Sure. What's your first name?"

"Lawrence," the boy replied.

"I like your name," Deandra remarked, which was true. At the same time, she was worried about thinking of three separate messages to write in each of the books! She was suddenly so nervous her mind went blank.

Meanwhile, Lawrence asked her, "Do you have a cat named Theo? Does he look like the one in the books you write?"

Deandra kept her eyes glued on the first message she was attempting to write on the inside cover of "Theo Guards the Hen House" and shook her head slightly, keeping her answer "no" purposely vague. Meanwhile, Lawrence's mother appeared and stood before her, too. They could decipher Deandra's response to the questions however they wanted. And tomorrow she was going to the local animal shelter and adopt herself a cat! He (or she) might not look anything like Theo the Cat, but it was a start!

About the Author

Amy has written several novels and short story collections, including a trio of books with off-beat dog themes. She lives on a horse farm in Indiana. AmyKristoff.com.

Printed in the USA
CPSIA information can be obtained
at www.ICGtesting.com
JSHW080738161123
51837JS00009B/16

9 781937 869212